+Published by:

Hollygrove Publishing, Inc.
4100 West Eldorado Parkway
Suite 100-182
McKinney, Texas 75070
(972) 837-6191
http://www.hollygrovepublishing.com

10 – digit ISBN, print ed.   0977793915
13 - digit ISBN, print ed.   9780977793914

Printed in the United States of America

Publisher's Note
This is a fictitious novel. All events in this story are solely the product of the Author's imagination. Any similarities between any characters and situations in this book to any individuals, living or dead, or actual places and situations are purely coincidental.

Mama's Lies - Daddy's Pain

By

Brian W. Smith

Acknowledgments

I'd like to acknowledge everyone who supported me and encouraged me to write this book.

I'd also like to use this book to give a long overdue "shout out" to all of the brotha's (African-American, Latino, Asian, and Caucasian) out there who work their asses off trying to be good dads. Those brotha's who don't quit their jobs and hide their addresses in an effort to avoid paying child support. Those brotha's who are actually enthusiastic about taking their children for the weekend and spending quality time with them. Those brotha's who hold off on purchasing the 20" rims and instead choose to put the money into their child's college fund. Those brotha's who actually attend their child's school functions. This book was written for those brotha's who are willing to put up with the "baby mama's" from hell - just so that they can remain an active participant in their child's life. To all of you brotha's out there who shatter the stereotypes, ignore the naysayers, and take being a "daddy" serious …this book was mainly written in honor of you!

Table of Contents

Introduction

I have a question for the women out there – what would you do if your girlfriend lied about the identity of her child's father? Would you be the moral compass in the situation and encourage her to tell the truth or would you laugh and turn the other cheek?

To the men out there I have a question – what would you do if your best friend were a deadbeat dad? Would you encourage him to be responsible or would you turn the other cheek and "mind your business?"

This book tackles two very important issues: the issue of scandalous "baby mama's" that lie, manipulate, and seem to think that the "ends" always justify the "means" when it comes to raising a child **and** deadbeat dads who give all fathers a bad name.

Calm down, calm down! Before you send your lynch mob out to find and hang me from the nearest tree, I ask that you relax and pause for a second. The truth of the matter is, what I describe in this book may not be anything that you'd do; however, we all have at least one friend, a family member, a sorority sister, a cousin, a fraternity brother, an uncle, or a co-worker who is guilty of doing some of the things the characters in this book have done.

The reason I wrote this book is to enlighten you (women and men) – give you some "game." So sit back and prepare to be schooled.

The Characters

Jamal Simms is a young, successful, entrepreneur. He has a beautiful wife, daughter, and son. He owns a 4,500 square foot home, has two Mercedes Benzes in the driveway, and money in the bank. He is active in his church, his community, and a sucker for needy family members. He is the type of man most women want to marry, and he lives the life most men wish they had. But, there is one thing he'd trade all of his success for...the comfort of knowing that his 18-year-old daughter Jada (from a previous relationship) is really his child.

Greg Johnson has been Jamal's best friend since high school. If you ask Greg how an unemployed man can live in a stylish Uptown townhouse, drive a Range Rover, and wear a Rolex watch, he'll tell you he invested his $250,000 insurance settlement wisely. The truth is, Greg is a "gigolo!" He's a bachelor who stands 6'4" tall, weighs a chiseled 215 pounds, wavy hair, hazel eyes, a skin complexion that is as smooth as caramel, and dimples that are deep enough for a woman to climb in and fall asleep. Based on his physical appearance and material possessions, he too is the type of man most women want to marry and lives the life most men wish they had. But, there is one disturbing fact about Greg that all the expensive cologne in the world can't cover up...he could be the poster boy for "deadbeat" dads.

Tracy Newhouse is the mother of Jamal's daughter. She is very smart and pretty, and on the surface appears to be of sound mind. But, when it comes to raising Jada...it's either her way or no way. As far as Tracy is concerned, Jamal has two roles in Jada's life: provide financial support and play "bad" cop when she needs him to. The only thing that's worse than her attitude is her secret...an eighteen-year-old secret.

Jada Simms is Jamal and Tracy's daughter. She loves both of her parents but she's torn. Often times her head sides with her dad, but her heart is in her mom's corner. She hates having to choose sides so she remains neutral on most issues. Her relationship with both of her parents is as complex as a maze. Unfortunately, Jada learns that sometimes in life trying to remain "neutral" can be worse than choosing sides.

Prologue

The death of a child can be devastating. It can trigger an emotional pain that only another parent can relate to. I didn't lose a child literally, but Jada's declaration that she's, _"Moved on to another phase of her life"_ symbolizes a figurative loss that I simply can't put into words.

Although rain drops the size of nickels pelted my windshield and made it difficult for me to see, I was still able to carefully maneuver my car out of the tight parking space at the deli. I used extreme caution as I drove back to this hotel room. My clothes and face are soaking wet from the rain. The water dripping from my face has to come from the rain because I still have the _"out of commission"_ sign on my tear ducts. Shit, I can't remember the last time I cried. Now that I think about it, I haven't cried since my mother's funeral two years ago. I'm still trying to process what just happened to determine if this situation is worth my tears.

This room seems to be getting smaller; or maybe I'm just hallucinating. I feel nauseous and I want to puke, but now isn't the time. I'm getting conflicting signals from my body. My stomach is doing flips, but my mind is preoccupied with other distasteful thoughts. I find myself calculating – not the amount of miles or time it took for me to drive to Louisiana, but the amount of emotional and monetary investment I made in Jada. I've spent the last eighteen years of my life providing emotional support to that child, and somewhere in the ballpark of $100,000 to make sure she always had everything she needed.

The analytical side of my personality has started to kick in, and I can't help but dissect the word "support." To fully understand the extent of my involvement in Jada's life; thus, my interpretation of the word "support" – you have to be able to overlook the financial aspect and identify with the scenes lurking in the corners of my mind – scenes such as: attending birthday parties, forcing myself to sit through dozens of animated movies, helping her with homework assignments and class projects, attending parent/teacher conferences, taking her on dinner dates to show her how a man should treat her, showering her with unsolicited compliments to help build her self-esteem, ensuring that she and her posse of friends made it to and from football games, trying to pretend I don't see boys flirting with her as we walked through the shopping mall, threatening to file a lawsuit against the school district if the school didn't control the girls who bullied her, trying to explain to her why love hurts, debating whether or not to issue a beat down to the boy who made her cry, taking her on tours of college campuses to introduce her to the joys of higher learning, saying a prayer for both of us before each driving lesson, having dancing contests in the living room, teaching her the difference between disrespect and a compliment, punishing her when she screwed up, and smothering her with hugs when she gave a valiant effort to succeed at any task. When I say support, I mean all of these things – not just the money.

Most men are like me; they take being a father serious. But there are some deadbeats who see things differently than I do and run from the pressure. I spent eighteen years trying to avoid the "deadbeat" title. Shit, the fact that I'm sitting here in this cramped hotel room is proof of my good intentions towards her. I thought coming here would make a difference. I guess this was my attempt at extending an "olive branch" – monumental mistake.

You had to be there to see the look on her face when she told me that I wasn't invited to her wedding. How can I not be invited to her wedding? I'm the person who spent nearly two decades robbing Peter to pay Paul so that she could have everything. I'm still shocked at the way she started talking on the phone, and acted as if I wasn't there. The way she reluctantly took the piece of paper that I wrote my hotel room and phone number on. The awkward stretches of silence were painful - it was as if we'd never known each other.

For some strange reason I'm starting to feel the need to remove that *"out of commission"* sign, and give my tear ducts a good work out. I can see the people on my television, but I can't hear what they are saying. The sounds of their voices are now muffled by the sound of my crying; crying that seems to travel with it's own orchestra - an orchestra that's anchored by moans and sniffling.

These sounds are foreign to me, but I know that they are real. They are as real as this grip I have on the pillow beneath my head, as I lay here on this lumpy ass bed in the fetal position. I'm feeling alone.

I'm feeling betrayed. I'm feeling like I don't deserve this. I'm feeling like I may have brought this on myself. I'm hearing the voices of my friends telling me to suck it up and "charge this shit to the game." I want to beat my chest and pretend what happened doesn't hurt, but I can't. I'm physically paralyzed and emotionally drained, and any attempts to muster up fabricated machismo are proving to be futile.

I could continue to describe this evening to you and my current emotional state as I lay here with my eyes blood shot red, but I won't do that. Actually, I think now would be a good time to tell you the entire story of how this rather pitiful scene came to be...

Chapter 1 - *Do The Right Thing*

Jamal

The summer of 1986 was shaping up to be pretty damn good for me. I was entering my senior year in high school, I didn't have a criminal record, and I hadn't fathered any kids. I didn't have a job, but the little money I earned from being the neighborhood barber was enough to keep me happy. As long as I could buy myself a few Ralph Lauren polo shirts and Bally tennis shoes, life was great.

When I wasn't goofing off with my friends or hanging out at the local shopping mall, I could usually be found hanging out at my girlfriend Tracy's house. Tracy was a tall, slim, and very attractive sophomore who attended a local all girl school. We met a year earlier, and started dating shortly thereafter.

To say that our relationship progressed quickly would be an understatement. Innocent hand holding scenes and trips to local theaters to see matinees were quickly replaced with unbridled public displays of affection and all night intimate phone conversations; conversations that usually ended with one of us falling asleep while holding the telephone.

At the tender ages of 16 and 14, Tracy and I thought we were grown, and it wasn't long before we were engaging in "grown folk" activity. We hadn't reached the four-month mark in the relationship when that unrelenting narcotic called *lust* mixed with our raging hormones. Before we knew it, innocent late night marathon phone conversations were replaced with perfectly orchestrated summer time "booty calls."

During our season of lewdness, I rarely used a condom and Tracy rarely insisted. Lust skewed our already poor judgment. Even a blind man could see that promiscuity would become our downfall.

In many ways, we weren't that different from many of the teenagers in neighborhoods across this sex craved nation. Our modus operandi was really very similar to the one used by many teenagers – yeah, maybe even your teenager - so pay close attention because the scenario is more prevalent than most parents realize.

During the summer months, parents would get up and go to work Monday thru Friday, and leave their horny ass teenage kids at home. In between accomplishing the various tasks written on the "Things To Do" list posted prominently on the refrigerator - teenage boys and girls across the city were sneaking their lovers in the house through windows, back doors, and down chimneys if need be. Tracy and I were no different.

After a day of sex, cereal, and soap operas, the clean-up process would usually begin at roughly two o'clock in the afternoon. For those of you who lived a more sheltered life and are unaware of the clean-up process - here is the cliff notes version of what it consisted of:

(1)   Taking a quick shower and then using a towel to wipe down the tub so that it appeared dry.

(2)   Washing and drying the sex stained bed sheets and putting them back on the bed.

(3)   Using a can of air freshener to eliminate the "boodussy" (that's booty-dick-pussy for the ebonically challenged) smell that seemed to insist on lingering in the air.

(4)   Placing the used condoms in a paper bag and putting them in the garbage can – outside.

(5)   Doing a thorough scan of the bedroom floor to make sure that no pieces of the condom wrapper had been overlooked and waiting to be found. Veterans to the game knew that the key was to never rip the top of the condom wrapper all the way off – just tear it enough to slide the condom out.

(6)   Calling a friend across the street and telling him/her to go outside and check for any signs of parental activity - if the coast was clear, the sex exhausted lover was sent on his/her way never to be seen or heard from again...that is until plans could be made to hook up again later on that week.

My family lived at the end of a newly developed subdivision. The walk from the bus stop to my house was approximately seven minutes. It was important to know the precise time because the buses were rarely late. If you missed the bus you'd be waiting thirty minutes for the next one to appear. Another reason why it was important to know the schedule was because it reduced the probability of you and your young lover having to stand at the bus stop – in the middle of the day - looking awkward and guilty.

At least two or three times a week Tracy and I would make our way to my house from the bus stop. As we walked past my friend's houses, I tried to pretend I didn't notice my buddies peeking out of their living room windows. Everyone in the neighborhood knew about "the walk." It even became a neighborhood competition amongst the boys to see who could have the most "walks" during the summer. Even the girls in the neighborhood would look out of their windows and shake their heads in pity as they watched another unsuspecting victim being led to some boy's home.

I'd won the neighborhood contest the previous summer with 14 "walks", and was trying to repeat as the champ – not an easy task now that Ricky Trufant lived up the street. Ricky was the new "cat" on the block. He had a light brown complexion with wavy hair. Ricky told everyone he had "Indian" in his family. All the girls called him "Pretty Ricky" – I called him a broke ass El DeBarge. Nonetheless, the girls loved him and he was definitely going to be my stiffest competition.

The threat of competing with Ricky Trufant didn't matter to me because Tracy's weekly visits all but guaranteed I would be the first on my block to repeat as the "walks" champion.

The competition was crazy. We ran the "walk" game like it was the NCAA tournament. We had strict rules and even a committee to judge the competition:

(1)   Everyone participating had to contribute ten dollars.

(2)   You had to be seen on the "walk" by at least two people.

(3)   You had to notify at least two people of an expected visit – no surprise "walks."

(4)   You had to show at least two people proof that you had sex – preferably the girl's panties, a picture or something.

That particular summer was special because we had ten guys signed up – five more than the previous year. The increased enrollment in our little friendly summer competition enabled us to up the ante. The winner would receive an unprecedented prize: fifty dollars cash, two free movie passes, and a dime bag of weed. The second place finisher got a box of condoms and one joint.

Our adolescent ignorance was never more recognizable than during this summer contest. Just to win that ridiculous first place prize, guys would have sex with anyone to increase their score. My next-door neighbor was a dude named *Jelly Bean*. He got the nickname Jelly Bean because that's all he ate. We could be playing football in the middle of the street and he would stop and pull a handful of sticky jellybeans out of his pocket. He even ate the black ones.

Jelly Bean was 16 years old and weighed nearly 300 lbs. He seemed to wear the same outfit everyday and was always funky. The boy was so funky that my mama told me he could never come back inside our house. He would have sex with his dog if he thought it would increase his "walks" total.

As the summer came to a close, Jelly Bean was still in last place. In an effort to get his score up, he befriended Ann Marie – a handicap girl that lived up the block. Ann Marie walked with a pronounced limp because her left leg was shorter than her right.

Before you start feeling sorry for Ann Marie let me tell you this, she didn't act like someone who had a handicap. Ann Marie would curse your as out in a heartbeat. On top of that, she was the biggest flirt in the neighborhood. She was actually kind of cute. She had a big butt and hazel eyes. There were guys who would comment on the size of her ass, but no one would touch her because of her handicap. Jelly Bean was the exception – he didn't care about her handicap. He could be seen at least twice a week doing the "walk" with Ann Marie. The mere thought of Jelly Bean rolling his big fat/funky ass on top of that short-legged girl kept us laughing.

Both of my parents were usually gone to work by eight o'clock every morning. I had a younger brother and sister, but neither of them dared to tell my parents I kept "company" during the summer. They both knew that I would beat the crap out of them if they opened their mouths. My mother worked at a hospital across town, and my dad worked at city hall, so the likelihood of them coming home during the day was slim.

I wasn't really worried about my dad finding out, but I was terrified that my mom might find about my escapades. I worshiped the ground my mother walked on. In my eyes she was the kindest person on the planet. She never missed a baseball or football game; she gave my siblings and I her last dime; she never belittled my dreams and aspirations – quite simply, she was the straw that stirred the drink in the Simms household. I viewed my mom as my alpha and omega.

Conversely, I viewed my father as the weight around all of our necks. Our relationship was about as unconventional as any father/son relationship could be. For years he emotionally abused my mother and me.

My father's teachings could only be described as "disgusting" by normal societal standards. Whether it was asking to borrow one of my condoms or making me relay messages to his numerous mistresses via the telephone - my father was the worst role model a boy could have. Rather than teach me how to be a man, he succeeded at teaching me the ropes on how to be a "playa"...and he seemed to take pride in it.

It's important that I take a moment to discuss my relationship with my father because it has a direct impact on the decisions I made throughout my life. As much as I hated the things he exposed me to, I secretly longed to receive his adoration. As a result, I spent as much time seeking his approval as I did wishing he'd go away.

I can remember when I was 15 years old, my dad asked me to go into the attic and retrieve some old football equipment that belonged to my younger brother. I obliged, and later asked him why he wanted the old equipment.

"I'll tell you later on this week," he replied.

Two days later, I watched him as he moved frantically throughout the house changing out of his work clothes, and into a pair of jeans and tennis shoes.

"Put on some shoes and let's take a ride," he said to me as he opened and closed the hallway closet.

As is the case with most boys, I yearned for any form of positive attention from my dad; therefore, the destination wasn't nearly as important as my dad's request that I join him.

Judging from the way I ran through the house trying to find my tennis shoes you would have thought the ice cream truck was parked outside giving away free "Nutty Buddies" and "Push-Ups." But, that wasn't the case; I was just a teenage boy enthralled by an unexpected invitation to accompany his father.

I ran to the passenger side of his car, and waited patiently for him to press the automatic door locks to open the door. My dad's car was a burgundy colored, 1981 Lincoln Continental Mark V – a poor man's Cadillac. The car had tan leather interior with automatic windows and locks, and even a little wood grain on the dashboard. It was far and away the nicest car anyone in my family owned. As a matter of fact, all of my older cousins always asked to borrow the car for proms and formal dances.

Whenever I was afforded the honor of riding in the car I felt like "ghetto royalty." I always hoped my friends were outside when I was in the front passenger seat so that I could give them the playa's head nod as I rode by. Unfortunately, the opportunity to showoff was rarely presented. Most of the time I found myself riding shotgun in my mama's green 1982 Ford Pinto.

As we pulled out of the driveway I couldn't help but wonder if my relationship with my dad was about to take a turn for the better. I smiled as I prepared myself for the stimulating father-and-son conversation that awaited me. This was what I'd been secretly wanting for years.

While driving down the long eastern New Orleans streets neither of us said a word. I had a million topics I wanted to bring up to break the silence, but I was afraid I might say something stupid. Rather than screw things up, I decided to remain quiet and enjoy the moment.

The huge magnolias trees that aligned the city's streets were picturesque, and as I stared out of the window at the beautiful scenery I begin to wonder about our final destination. Was my dad taking me to get that new pair of Bally tennis shoes I'd asked for a few weeks earlier? It was hot outside so maybe we were going to get some sno-balls. Nah, that couldn't be it, I couldn't remember the last time I'd seen my dad eat a sno-ball. I thought that maybe we were going to go and check out a movie at the new movie theatre on the service road across from the Lake Forest Plaza shopping center. My mind was all over the place as I wondered where our journey would end. Finally, I broke down and asked, "Where are we goin'?"

"You'll see when we get there," he replied in a tone that suggested I should just sit back and shut up.

My dream of doing something fun with him ended when he abruptly turned into the parking lot of a park located approximately ten minutes from our house. The parking lot was surrounded by trees and bushes, and seemed to be out of place. I looked around and noticed that our car couldn't be seen from the main street. I got out of the car with a bewildered look on my face. I remember thinking to myself:

I should have known he was up to something - this nigga gonna kill me and dump my body in these damn bushes.

I watched him as he got out of the car, and walked down a small trail that extended from the parking lot into the tree line.

"Come on boy – move like you got a purpose," he turned around and yelled.

I didn't respond but I know the look on my face said, *fuck you!* A few seconds passed and I eventually summoned the courage to follow him into the tree line. When I arrived on the other side of the trees I was surprised to see little kids running in the distance wearing shoulder pads and helmets that appeared to be way too big on most of them.

I smiled as I watched the kids run, fall, and cry on the massive make shift football field. My dad and I made our way towards the bleachers, and sat next to a man who was screaming as if he was at an NFL game. The man was cheering for a kid who was running down the sideline towards the end zone. The loud man stopped cheering and started cursing as he watched the boy get chased down and tackled by another little boy. The tackle was pretty impressive, and I found myself smiling as I marveled at the future Hall-of-Famers.

Out of the corner of my eye I could see that my dad was smiling uncontrollably. Sensing he was being watched, he leaned over and nudged me on the shoulder.

"You see that little boy that just made that tackle?" he asked.

"Yeah, what about him?" I replied.

My dad paused for a moment as he contemplated his next choice of words.

"That boy is your little brother," he whispered into my ear.

The first thought that came to my mind was: *I'll be damned!* But I couldn't say that. The only thing I could do was sit there with a stunned look on my face. One glance at me and he knew that this wasn't going to unfold the way he'd planned.

I shook my head in disbelief as I sat on the bleachers in the 90-degree temperature wondering why he'd brought me out there to show me that. I could feel the tension building in my shoulders as I became overwhelmed by what was transpiring.

My dad left the bleaches and walked over to the edge of the football field. He started talking to a slim dark complexioned lady with long hair - I assumed she was the little boy's mother. Seemingly from out of nowhere, the little boy appeared and leaped into my dad's arms; he was wearing the same helmet and shoulder pads that I'd retrieved from the attic earlier that week.

I immediately left the bleachers and started walking towards the car. My emotions were scattered like the pieces to a jigsaw puzzle. I had mixed emotions - one part of me was furious while the other part of me was left wondering if this was really happening. I knew he was a womanizer, but at no time did I ever think about the possibility that he may have fathered other children.

As I approached the car I looked around at the park and the surrounding neighborhood. I kept asking myself if this was real. An unexpected summer breeze hit my face causing me to snap out of my temporary trance and back to reality. This was no daydream – my father had just informed me that I had a half brother. That little boy couldn't have been more than six years old. My younger sister and brother were eleven and ten years old.

What was I supposed to do with that information? I couldn't tell my mother because it would crush her. I couldn't tell my siblings because they were still too young to grasp the situation. I couldn't tell any of my friends because they would only make fun of me behind my back and some would laugh in my face.

Yep, when it came to playing the "dozens" nothing was off limits in my circle of friends and I knew it; therefore, divulging my secret to even my closest friends was out of the question. Armed with that type of information they would come after me like a shark in pursuit of a bleeding swimmer. I could only imagine the type of jokes that would have come my way:

What's tall and black and got more mouths to feed than a homeless shelter...Jay's daddy!

What's black and long, and just filed for workers comp because it's been overworked... Mr. Simm's dick!

What's that black square thing running down the street
trying to get away from that white dude...Jay's
daddy's wallet running from the child support man.

Oh hell no! There was no way on earth I was going
to tell anyone about this.

I leaned against the car and waited on him for
seemingly an hour (it was really ten minutes). Finally,
my dad emerged from the trees and walked towards
me with his trademark cocky swagger.

"Why did you walk away without saying hello to
your little brother?"

"Does mama know?"

"No she doesn't know, and she'd better not find
out," he responded as he gave me a look that
suggested he just might dump my ass in those bushes
at the park if I snitched on him.

He paused and lit a cigarette, shifted the car into
drive, and slowly drove out of the parking lot. He
stared straight ahead and avoided any eye contact
with me. I sat there quietly and tried to figure out why
he'd dropped this bombshell on me. What did he gain
from showing me this? I couldn't understand why he
kept using me as some type of receptacle for all of his
skeletons, guilt, and unwanted baggage.

Neither of us said a word for the duration of the
ride. As we pulled into our driveway, he turned to me
and asked, "Don't you want to know your little
brother's name?"

"No, you keep it!" I replied, and got out of the car.

We never spoke of the little boy again, and I never
mentioned it to my mother. That day served as the
turning point in our relationship. I despised him for
saddling me with such an emotional burden, and
hoped everyday that he would just pack his bags,
leave, and never come back.

Ironically, it was my devotion to my mother that forced me to keep my dad's wrong doings hidden. Hurting my mom was not an option; therefore, I did what I thought was best during that time – I kept quiet about what I'd seen and blurred my thoughts with a cloud of weed smoke.

By the end of the summer of 1986, that childhood desire to spend any form of quality time with my father was non-existent. I was almost seventeen years old and I no longer cared.

As time went on, my lack of respect for him started to show more and more. He came home from work early a few times during that summer, and caught Tracy and me in my bedroom. I barely acknowledged his presence and he never commented.

My dad wasn't crazy. He knew Tracy and I had been screwing like rabbits, but what could he say - he had a mistress in every part of the city and I suspect a few babies to go with them. Circumstances dictated that he left me alone. The only thing I had to worry about was getting Tracy out of the house in time so that she could make it back to her house before four o'clock – that's when her mom got home from work.

Shortly after the 4th of July, I decided to start getting prepared for my senior year. I cleaned out my closet to make room for the new stuff I intended to buy. To sponsor my addiction to designer clothes I increased my haircut clientele and the cost of haircuts. A regular hair cut which was once seven dollars was increased to eight dollars. The cost for a fancy design such as the Louis Vutton logo or a martini glass was increased from ten dollars to twelve.

I usually cut hair on my parents back patio. Rarely did I ask my parents for money; therefore they didn't complain about the large crowds of boys waiting to get haircuts. All they asked was that I cleaned up the hair and kept my noisy friends outside.

Once I'd earned enough money to get all of the school clothes I wanted, there was only one thing left for me to do to get ready for my senior year...breakup with Tracy!

It was July 28th, and I was all prepared to kick Tracy to the curve. I'd spent all day thinking about my break-up speech. Periodically throughout the day I could be seen soliloquizing:

Tracy you know I care about you, but it's my senior year and I need to focus on school. I need to get ready for life after high school, and I need to work on my grades so I can get a scholarship or some shit. A brotha just need some space. We can hook up from time to time, but I need to be on my own.

I was standing in front of the mirror rehearsing like an actor preparing for an audition when the phone rang.

"Hello."

"Are you busy?" Tracy asked.

"Actually, I was just about to call you...we need to talk."

Tracy was silent for a moment, but before I could ask her what was wrong she let me know.

"My period is late!" she blurted out.

I could feel my heart rate speed up. I scratched my forehead as I searched for a response. After a few seconds passed I finally said the same ignorant shit most boys (and men) say, "Why are you tellin' me?"

"I'm tellin' you because I might be pregnant!" Tracy yelled.

I could feel my stomach starting to get queasy. I sat on a chair and begin to think about possible reasons why her period could be late. My search for an explanation proved to be useless, so I quickly switched my thoughts to ways of getting that damn period out of her.

"My mama once told me that if a girl drinks hot tea or coffee it might help it come down," I said, while trying to remain cool.

By this time, Tracy could no longer contain her emotions. She became frantic as she tried explaining all that she'd done to try to get her monthly visitor to appear.

"I've been tryin' everything Jay."

"Well you'd better try somethin' else. Go run around the block or do some jumping jacks or go sit on the toilet and take a long hard shit. All I know is that you'd better do somethin' because I ain't tryin' to be a daddy."

I slammed the phone down on the receiver and went into my room. As feelings of anger and fear surged through me, I started contemplating the possibility of having to support a child. To make matters worse, I didn't want to deal with Tracy anymore – hell, I was preparing to break up with her when she called. Nevertheless, it seemed foul to break up with her knowing that she was pregnant. I was trapped.

I wanted to turn to GOD for help, but felt uncomfortable because my family wasn't very religious. As a matter of fact, I couldn't remember the last time we'd all attended a church service as a family. I can remember going on Easter Sunday a few times, but it had been years since we'd done that.

Even so, I got on my knees and tried to say any prayer I could think of. I was terrible at praying, but I'd heard GOD was omnipotent; therefore, I figured GOD would have no problem deciphering my sorry attempt at prayer:

Our Father, who art in heaven, thou kingdom come, thou will be done, on earth as it is in heaven. Lord please don't let this girl be pregnant. Now I lay me down to sleep, I pray the Lord my soul to keep - GOD is great - GOD is good, so deliver us from evil, and forgive us of our sins. Lord please don't let this girl be pregnant. Lead us not into temptation, but forgive us our trespassers as we forgive those who mess over us and be trippin'. Lord I don't care what you do to me, just please don't let this girl be pregnant. In the name of the father, the son, and the holy spirit... Lord pleeeeease don't let this girl be pregnant. Hail Mary, Hallelujah, and Amen.

I spent the next two days trying to earn some brownie points with GOD. I turned my radio on the gospel station and let it stay there all day. By the second day, I was actually learning the words to a few songs. Truth be told, there were a few that I actually liked. I actually said my prayers before I ate, and made the sign of a cross whenever I passed any church or religious house of worship – Catholic, Baptist, Jewish synagogues, and even Nation of Islam temples – I didn't care.

I avoided Tracy's phone calls during that time, but thanks to my younger sister, she was finally able to contact me three days later. In true annoying little sister fashion, she told Tracy that I was home. I gave my sister a slap upside the head as I took the phone from her. I took a deep breath and prepared myself for the worst.

"Hello!" I said not bothering to hide my desire to be left alone.

"Hey Jamal! Where have you been the last two days?" Tracy asked in a confrontational tone. "I've been tryin' to call you."

I rolled my eyes and looked up at the ceiling. I wanted her to cut to the chase, but I reluctantly dealt with the small talk.

"Yeah I know. I've been busy trying to make some money."

"Whatever! You've been avoiding me!" Tracy yelled. "All I wanted to tell your ass was that my period came down. I'm not pregnant."

I damn near dropped the phone. I was happier than a contestant on the Price Is Right. I looked up at the ceiling and silently mouthed, *Thank you GOD!* After a few seconds of silently rejoicing, I pulled myself together and responded in the calmest voice that I could muster up.

"I figured it would. I knew you were just getting' nervous over nothing. I was chillin' – I wasn't worried bout that."

"Yeah right," Tracy mumbled. "When am I gonna see you again Jamal?"

I cringed at the question. I was so happy she wasn't pregnant that I forgot parts of the breakup speech I'd been rehearsing. I cleared my throat and in my most serious tone I attempted to recite as much of my breakup speech as I could remember.

"Tracy – it's over!" I announced and hung up the phone. As you can see, my speech didn't quite come out the way I planned, but when you're a 16-year-old boy waiting for the results of a pregnancy test, the only thing you care about are the words "I'm not pregnant."

The scare of my life was finally over and it was time to focus on being a senior. No harm, no foul. I could move on and so could she. With the exuberance and joy of a child awakening on Christmas Day, I ran through the house yelling. Eventually I ended up in my bedroom jumping on my bed.

Later on that evening I hooked up with my friends and was awarded my first place prize for the "walk" contest. I finished with 17 walks that summer, four better than Jelly Bean's nasty ass. Ricky Trufant was stricken with the chicken pox midway thru the summer – he came in last place with 6 "walks."

My senior year was in full swing, and I loved every minute of it. Between football games, dances, and house parties seemingly every other weekend, I didn't have much time to give Tracy a second thought. I'd heard rumors that she'd been seen hanging out with different dudes, and starting to get a reputation for being "easy." My standard response to the rumors was, "So!"

As far as I was concerned Tracy was yesterday's newspaper. I had already met a new sophomore named Dawn, and she was so fine that all I could think about was getting closer to her. Besides, I always felt that it didn't matter who Tracy was dating because if I wanted her back all I had to do was call and she'd come running.

As it turned out, I wouldn't have to make that phone call to Tracy. In October of 1986 she called me.

"Whats up Jamal - are you busy?"

I was surprised to hear from Tracy. We hadn't talked since our break up three months earlier.

"No, I'm just layin' here watchin' television. What's up?"

Tracy paused for several seconds. I could sense something was wrong so I sat upright on the couch. I wasn't sure, but it sounded like she was crying.

"Tracy what's wrong? Are you crying?"

"Jay I'm pregnant!"

The first thing that crossed my mind was our conversation a few months earlier when she told me that her period had come. I felt bad for her, but I was relieved the baby wasn't mine. I attempted to console Tracy.

"Damn Tracy, I'm sorry to hear that. Don't worry about it, everything's gonna be alright. I know we've been on "bad terms", but I will help you anyway I can. Whose the daddy?" I asked in my most consoling voice.

"You!" Tracy responded.

Suddenly I felt a pain streak up my spine and my ass cheeks puckered as I jumped to my feet.

"Bullshit!" I yelled. "I haven't seen your black ass since the beginning of July. Besides, the last time we talked you said your period came down."

"It did come down, but I was still pregnant. Jamal, a woman can be pregnant and still have her period," Tracy said as she burst into tears.

Confused doesn't begin to describe my mental state. What I was experiencing probably qualified as outright panic. I started pacing back and forth and mumbling, "This ain't right. This aint right."

"What do you mean this ain't right? You know we were having sex all this summer," Tracy interjected.

I knew I couldn't argue that point because everybody in the "hood" knew Tracy and I had spent the entire summer sexing like porn stars. Shit, I'd won the neighborhood "walk" contest as a result of her frequent visits. Trying to downplay that fact would have been a waste of time. All of a sudden, winning that damn bag of weed and fifty dollars didn't seem so important.

Deep down I knew Tracy's call was suspicious, but I'd heard that some women get pregnant and still have their periods. As much as I wanted to hang up in her face, I still believed that I was the only one sexing Tracy that summer...at least that's what I wanted to believe. Why shouldn't I believe it? Tracy hadn't given me any reason to think that she was sleeping with someone else. She claimed to be madly in love with me, and she told me so at least ten times a day. However, the fact still remained that I hadn't seen her in four months. Something wasn't adding up, but I wasn't quite sure.

Just as I was about to challenge her accusation, Tracy's mom got on the phone, and asked to speak to my dad. Initially I was surprised so I stopped talking for a few seconds and contemplated whether or not to give the phone to him. My hesitation had nothing to do with my fear of his reaction. I was actually hesitant because I wasn't sure how the discussion between the two of them would turn out.

Earlier that year, I'd found out that my dad had hooked up with Tracy's mom. Apparently, their paths crossed while partying one night at a local nightspot where the 35 and older crowd hung out. Tracy's mom and my dad went back to her apartment. While they sat in the living room, Tracy came downstairs to go to the kitchen. She heard voices so she peeked into the living room before entering and that's when Tracy saw that the man her mom brought home from the club was her boyfriend's father.

Tracy called me the next day, and told me what she'd seen. I was angry about what I'd heard, but I never told my mom. I attempted to talk to my dad about it, but he seemed to find the coincidence much too amusing to have a serious discussion. I decided to store this incident in the same emotional closet with the other baggage I had been forced to carry.

Now Ms. Newhouse was on the phone asking to speak to my dad regarding an issue that was far more serious than their little rendezvous.

Despite my anxiety about the two of them talking, I couldn't say no. I went into my parent's bedroom, and asked my dad to step into the living room. As he came towards the door I whispered that it was Tracy's mom on the phone, and watched his facial expression. Initially, he thought I was hooking something up between the two of them so he smirked. But, it wasn't long before his grin turned into a look of fear. I turned and walked away, but I could hear my dad asking those questions every parent wishes to avoid:

"How do you know it's his?"

PAUSE

"How do you know she wasn't sleeping with someone else?"

PAUSE

"We're gonna have a blood test done, and I'm telling you right now, Jamal ain't marrying her."

My dad was pretty animated at that point. He hung up the phone, and walked past me without making eye contact. He went back into his bedroom, and slammed the door behind him. A few minutes later, both of my parents came out. The look on my dad's face said it all. I already knew what he was going to ask before he opened his mouth.

"Are you sure it's yours?"

"Yeah!"

"Jamal, why didn't you wear a rubber?" he asked with a look of exasperation.

I didn't bother replying because I instinctively knew the question was rhetorical. The look that my dad gave me was that of a man who felt his son had just thrown his life away.

My mama was never a big disciplinarian so she just stood there quietly with tears in her eyes. As my dad turned and walked away, mama approached me shaking her head. She gave me a hug and walked back into her bedroom.

After that night there were never any other discussions about having a blood test. If there was ever a time when my dad should have taken control of a situation and made me do something, it was then. I suspect his reluctance to preach to me about the error of my ways had a lot to do with his own secrets.

Deep down I knew Tracy's claim was questionable, but my pride wouldn't let me tell my dad about how Tracy had suddenly changed her story. In my mind, to admit that Tracy told me something different just a few months earlier would be admitting that she may have been sleeping around on me. It would have suggested that I wasn't smart enough to realize I was getting "played."

Before I would allow myself to look weak in front of my dad, I felt I could save face by keeping quiet...which is arguably the most immature and ignorant choice I've ever made.

I really needed some moral support, so I left and went to my best friend Greg's house. Greg's mom was a flight attendant and was rarely at home. Greg and I spent a lot of time hanging out in his bedroom smoking weed and sipping on everything from Boones Farm to Mad Dog 20/20 to that Pink Chablis wine that came in the big green glass container.

To describe Greg as "rough around the edges" would be an understatement...diplomacy was not his forte. Greg had a habit of being brutally honest. He'd tell his grandmother her breath stunk if the situation presented itself. When I told him about Tracy's pregnancy he was true to form.

Greg sat quietly on the bed with a shoebox on his lap. He gave me his undivided attention and listened intently to my story. While I talked, Greg slowly opened the box and began separating the marijuana leaves from the stems. His face was emotionless as he pulled out his pack of zig-zags and started rolling a joint. Greg's concentration was equal to that of a heart surgeon in surgery. After he finished rolling the joint Greg looked at me and said, "Nigga you just witnessed joint rolling at its highest level. I should charge your ass a fee for lettin' you watch me."

After marveling at his perfectly rolled joint for a few seconds, Greg lit it and took a long puff. He sat there for a moment and savored the flavor – the boy was serious about his weed. He reluctantly passed the joint to me, and watched carefully to make sure I didn't drop it or slob too much; thus, ruining all of his hard work.

Greg closed his eyes and leaned against the head board. He stared at me for a few moments and then asked, "Dog, you do realize that bitch is lying don't you?"

After taking a long puff on the joint (which had to be as fat as anything Cheech and Chong ever rolled), I responded, "It's gotta be mine because I'm the only person who was hittin' it."

Greg started laughing uncontrollably. It took him a few seconds to regain his composure.

"Man if you think you were the only person hittin' that, then your ass is dumber than you look."

"What you tryin' to say?" I asked, as my face filled with frown lines.

"Nigga I'm trying to say just what I said! You're crazy if you believe that. You told me yourself she was supposedly seeing that dude Sean at school. Just last week my homeboy over at Riverside High School said he heard Tracy was kickin' it with some dude over there. I think he said the dude played in the band or some shit."

"If you knew about some dude at Riverside why didn't you tell me?" I yelled.

"I didn't tell you because I didn't think it mattered. All your ass talk about these days is that new chick Dawn you've been messin' with," Greg yelled back.

We spent the next hour smoking weed and listening to L.L. Cool J's song "I'm Bad" and Eric B and Rakim's song "Paid in Full" over and over again.

The irony of it all was that both of those songs were the direct opposite of my current situation. I wasn't feeling "BAD" at the time, and the fact that I didn't have the money to pay Greg the $20 dollars I'd borrowed two weeks earlier proved that I damn sure wasn't "Paid In Full."

As our high started to wear off later on that night the reality of my situation settled in. I was going to be a father, and I couldn't even take care of myself.

Three months later, Tracy gave birth to a beautiful 6 pound little girl. I wasn't in the room during Jada's birth because Tracy's family was there, and I was scared they'd attack me. After all, I was the terrible young man that had impregnated their precious Tracy.

For most of that day I stayed at home near the phone, and waited for Tracy to call and tell me that the coast was clear. When she did finally call, I dashed out of the door and ran to the bus stop.

I arrived at the hospital about six hours after Jada's birth carrying a flimsy flower arrangement that I'd stolen from off of the counter in the hospital's lobby. There were signs within the first twenty-four hours of Jada's life that Tracy and I would have a problem sharing parental responsibilities.

"How are you doing?"

"I'm fine. I'm just feeling sore," Tracy responded, grimacing as she attempted to sit up.

"I can understand that you just pushed something the size of a bowling ball out of your body. Where is my baby?"

"She's right there in the basinet."

It wasn't until I looked at Jada for the first time that I realized the magnitude of my responsibility. She was tiny – smaller than the length of a football. Her tiny little hands and feet didn't look real. Her skin complexion and the texture of her hair made her look like a little Mexican baby.

"She doesn't bite, pick her up," I heard Tracy whisper.

I reached down and picked her up. My hands were shaking uncontrollably. I'd never held a baby this small, and I kept hoping that I wouldn't drop her.

As I stood there holding Jada, she opened her tiny little eyes and gave me an interesting look. It was as if she was trying to say with her eyes, *Nigga you'd better take care of me!*

Whether she was trying to say that or not, that's what I was thinking. I looked at my baby and started talking to her.

"Hey Nia, how are you doing baby?" I asked.

"Oh yeah, I forgot to tell you, her name isn't Nia," Tracy commented with an uncomfortable look on her face. I couldn't tell if the look was the result of her labor experience or her underhanded decision to change the child's name.

"What do you mean her name isn't Nia, that's the name we chose two days ago?"

"Well, I thought about it and decided to name her Jada."

"Oh really! So, you don't think you should have told me?"

Before she could answer my question a nurse came into the room, and started checking on the baby and Tracy. The nurse looked as if she was old enough to be our mother. She was a huge light skinned woman with short hair and a thin mustache. The woman seemed kind of mean. She flung pillows aside and moved covers with more aggression than necessary.

"So Tracy, is this little Jada's father?"

"Yeah, that's Jamal. Jamal this is Nurse Betty – she knows my mama."

"Hello," I said reluctantly. Her body language told me that she had a problem with me.

"Hello," she responded without looking at me. And then she asked, "Have you signed the birth certificate?"

"No, I didn't know I had to."

"This is your baby right? Well then, you need to sign the birth certificate and give this child your last name."

I looked at Nurse Betty and thought to myself:

You big mustache wearing woman, I didn't do a damn thing to you. Why do you have an attitude with me?

When Nurse Betty finished doing whatever she was pretending to be doing, she walked passed me and whispered in my ear, "Tracy's a good child, you make sure you take care of that baby."

By that time I was pissed, so I looked at Nurse Betty and replied, "I'ma take care of mine don't worry about that!" I then reached into my pocket and pulled out some peppermints and offered her one. I knew she caught the hint because she rolled her eyes at me and walked out of the room. I didn't care if she was mad, she was out of line and I wanted her to know it.

I figured the argument about Jada's name could wait until after Tracy got out of the hospital. I signed Jada's birth certificate, and started thinking about more important issues – like how my life was about to change forever.

Everyone was happy at the site of the beautiful child, but things were getting tense behind the scenes. First, my relationship with Dawn was becoming more and more intense. Dawn was a knockout. She had beautiful caramel skin, sexy eyes, a beautiful smile, the body of a stripper, and a pleasant personality. She also had the type of swagger I like (not too ghetto, but just enough "hood" in her to hold my interest). She also had a religious foundation that all guys want their girlfriends to have. I was smitten from the moment I met her.

Dawn felt the same way about me...until Jada was born. After much deliberation and some perfectly placed doubt by some of her meddlesome girlfriends, she decided to break up with me.

As much as she tried to be the ideal girlfriend the fact still remained that she was only 15, and had no desire to deal with someone else's baby. After pleading with Dawn to be more understanding, I decided to give her some space. The more I thought about it, the more I was fine with her decision. I liked her, but at the moment I had much bigger fish to fry. Time apart was what we both needed, and we wisely took it.

Back at home, the tension between my dad and I was at an all time high. I could see that he was tempted to give me a lecture, but wouldn't because he had no room to criticize. Watching my dad battle his moral demons was funny to me. Despite his inability to chastise me, he still had no problem making his position clear regarding financial support. Every chance he got he'd remind me of the financial crisis that loomed over my head like a dark rain cloud.

"Jamal, how are you gonna take care of that baby?"

"I got a job yesterday at Universal Supermarket," I defiantly responded.

My dad chuckled and sarcastically asked, "You think that supermarket job and cutting hair is gonna support a new baby? Your mama and I aren't gonna take care of your responsibility. I don't know what you're gonna do, but you're gonna have to be a man and take care of that child."

I didn't know if I was more pissed at what my dad said or how he said it. After all, I wasn't stupid; I knew

that $4 an hour wasn't going to go far. By the second
month on my new job I was already feeling the
financial crunch. Between giving Tracy a little money,
and my immature desire to buy clothes for myself,
that little "grocery bagger" paycheck was gone quicker
than I could say my name. I knew that I had to do
something else to make some more money. Two of my
fellow grocery baggers and I devised a scheme.

Along with bagging customer groceries and
retrieving run away baskets, the supermarket required
all baggers to take a customer's groceries to their car.
An additional duty of ours was to restock the shelves
with all items that had been randomly discarded
throughout the store. Customers would often change
their minds about purchasing certain items once they
arrived at the register. Those items that weren't
purchased would be placed into one of our restock
baskets, and put back on the shelves at the end of the
day. We all hated restocking...until we figured out a
way to incorporate it into our hustle.

Since the baggers like myself were usually in the
front of the store and clearly visible, our hustle had to
be incorporated into our everyday responsibilities. On
Saturdays when the supermarket was the busiest, I
would wait until the managers weren't looking and
then place bags of diapers and baby formula in those
restock baskets. Whenever a customer came through
the line with a lot of groceries I would bag his/her
groceries, and let the customer push their own basket
out. I would also bag the items that had been piling
up in the restock basket, and without the customers
realizing what was happening I would follow them out
of the store pushing the restock basket myself. I would
follow the customer close enough to give the
impression to anyone looking that the basket I was
pushing belonged to the customer. Once I exited the
store I would detour towards the side of the store and
leave the basket sitting on the side of the building. I

would help the customers put their groceries in the car and return to the store immediately. One of my fellow baggers (who would conveniently be out in the parking lot collecting discarded baskets) would go over and grab the items out of the basket and put them into his car. After work we would all split up the items we'd stolen. All I wanted was pampers, formula, and baby food. The other guys usually took all of the food and drinks. I would bring the stuff I stole to Tracy's house, which was located around the corner from the supermarket.

This little hustle saved me hundreds of dollars in diaper and formula expenses, but did very little to improve my overall economic status. I had to do something and I had to do it fast.

One night, Greg and I sat in his backyard and smoked a "clicker". In New Orleans a clicker is a joint dipped in embalming fluid. You have two kinds of clickers – dry or wet. The dry clickers were usually wrapped in aluminum foil and placed in the freezer for a few minutes – they were potent. The wet clickers were the worst – those were smoked with the fluid still dripping off them. We stuck with the dry clickers because we weren't trying to go crazy...in hindsight we were already crazy. Either form of clicker was dangerous. A few puffs and most people would "click" out, hence the name "clicker."

I took a long puff of this unusually fat clicker Greg had prepared for our smoking pleasure. I looked at him and then unveiled my plan for taking care of my beautiful daughter Jada.

"Dog, next month I'm gonna go into the Marines."

I made my announcement just as Greg was taking a long puff on the "clicker." Greg was so shocked, he started choking and laughing at the same time.

"Man I knew you couldn't handle this "fire" weed...you startin' to say some dumb shit."

"No dog, I'm serious," I replied.

"Why you wanna join the Marines? Who you think you are - Rambo? They gonna call your black ass RAMBRO!"

"Man I gotta take care of my daughter, and my old man is starting to act funny with me. I gotta get out of that house."

"Man if your pops is trippin' you can come live here. My mama won't mind; shit, I think she likes your ass more than she like me."

Suddenly, Greg pulled out a 38-caliber revolver, and aimed it at me.

"You're around here gettin' people pregnant – if you come and live here you'd better not try to fuck my mama. You get my mama pregnant and I'ma shoot your ass."

My first reaction was to laugh, but I quickly remembered that we were smoking "clickers" so I shut up. I didn't want Greg to say something crazy and make Greg mad – he might really shoot.

Greg and I stared at each other for what seemed like an hour. Suddenly we both burst into laughter.

"Man that's why I don't like smokin' this shit with you – your ass is crazy." I said as I took a deep breath.

"Nigga, you were so scared you had slob hanging from your bottom lip. You looked like a runaway slave that just got caught," Greg replied as he laughed hysterically.

I chuckled as I realized Greg was right. Actually, I was more scared than that slave Greg described. We spent the rest of the night looking up at the stars in the sky. Within one hour of that last puff we were both asleep in the backyard. We didn't awaken until the next morning when the neighbor's dog started barking.

By daybreak my weed high had worn off, but my problem still existed...I needed money. Greg moved around in his chair trying to find that comfort spot. Suddenly his eyes opened and he looked at me.

"Man was I trippin' last night or did you really say you were joinin' the Marines?"

"You heard right dog."

"Man you gotta be playin'?" asked Greg as he searched for his gun - it had fallen in the creases of the old recliner he was sitting in.

"Nah, dog I'm serious. I need some money! Are you gonna help me take care of her?"

"Hell no I ain't helpin' you take care of a baby! Besides, you talkin' about joinin' the Marines to take care of a baby, and you still don't know if that baby is yours. You should've taken a blood test to make sure because I still think Tracy is lying."

"Why are you so convinced she's lying? You know how much I was hittin' that this past summer."

"No disrespect dog, but I saw that baby. Your ass is darker than a nigga from Zimbabwe, and that baby is lighter than me...somethin' ain't right."

"So what! All babies are light skinned when they're born," I replied as I looked at Greg with disgust.

"That's true, but you still haven't explained to me how she was supposed to be four months pregnant when she first told you last October, and then the baby was born in January. I know you dumb, but you ain't that damn *ignant*. If that baby had been that premature the baby would still be in the hospital. First, her period was down while she was pregnant, and then she had a premature baby. You a bigger man than me dog because I would have told her to kiss my ass. I'm tellin' you, that girl is playin' you."

Sometimes Greg could be annoying the way he would go on and on about issues, but in this particular case I felt he was on to something. Tracy pretended to be crazy about me, but I had been hearing more and more rumors about the guy she was supposedly dating that went to Riverside High School. I chose to ignore the rumors because I didn't have any solid proof only hearsay - now I'm a daddy.

Like Spike Lee's popular movie, I felt that I had to *"Do The Right Thing!"* Unfortunately, trying to raise a child off of grocery bagger wages wasn't cutting it. As much as I didn't want to join the military, I felt it was my only "legal" alternative – so that's what I did.

Chapter 2 - *Mama's Point Of View*

Tracy

It wasn't long before all of the horror stories I'd heard about being a teenage parent started to come true. I was struggling to maintain my dignity, focus, and faith. Like so many girls who have babies at an early age, I placed my hopes, dreams, and life on hold to raise my child. I embarked on a journey that brought me down a road that had been often traveled, but not without its share of roadblocks.

Jamal and I had gone through our share of problems. Our disposition towards each other changed as often as the weather in the city we were both born and raised in. To say our relationship had its share of ebbs and flows would be an understatement. Sometimes we enjoyed being around each other – other times we didn't. Sometimes we looked at each other like the passion had never left – other times we looked at each other like murder was the next logical step. Sometimes we agreed on what was best for Jada – most of the time we didn't.

I believe Jamal thought that I was dumb or incapable of being a good mother. I knew I was extremely smart, and capable of doing great things – I didn't need his reassurance. I knew I was college material, but I had to put my dreams on hold.

It seems like we were always arguing about Jada or money. He accused me of deliberately trying to make him suffer because he started dating Dawn, but that had nothing to do with my anger towards him. My issue with him centered on the fact that I knew he could do more for Jada than he did. Jamal's biggest problem was that he spent more time worrying about material possessions than he did our child.

My background was pretty messed up. I didn't grow-up with the everyday influences of a positive male figure in the household. Both of my parents died before I turned five years old. My brothers and I were sent to live with different family members. That's how I ended up living with my aunt – commonly referred to as my mom.

It was tough on me at first because my aunt had her own kids, but she received me with open arms and gave me lots of love and support. My adopted sisters and brother treated me like I was their biological sibling. But, there is no replacement for a blood bond, and sometimes I felt like I was a burden. Getting pregnant at sixteen only compounded my insecurity.

I moved out of my mom's house shortly after my eighteenth birthday. Jada was two years old by then. It was around that time I learned that too many "women" in one house can be a problem. Although it was hard, I found a way to get my own place.

With the help of government assistance I got a cheap one-bedroom efficiency apartment, and furnished it with inexpensive but stylish furniture I'd purchased from a neighborhood furniture store. It was in that setting that my bond with Jada grew. We slept in the same bed, ate off of the same plates, drank from the same two cups, took baths together, and daydreamed together. I have no idea what she thought about, but it seems like my every thought revolved around the notion that things would get better.

As we lay in bed at night, I would often stare at the ceiling with Jada nestled comfortably up against my body. Big-ticket items like a car and private school were the furthest from my mind. I was more concerned about acquiring the simple necessities that many people take for granted – like a washing machine and dryer, a job that paid more than $6 an hour, a baby sitter other than my family members – all of whom were starting to tell me no more and more.

Jada attended daycare during the day, while I attended alternative school. Eventually, I got my G.E.D, but I soon learned another valuable lesson - a G.E.D. may help you get a job, but it usually doesn't coincide with having a career – so my first job was in the cutthroat world of fast food.

Jamal never gave a damn about how it made me feel to sit back and watch him graduate high school while I was forced to drop out. He escaped the crime-riddled city everyone calls the "Big Easy" and left me and his child trapped in mediocrity. During the first two years of Jada's life he "played" daddy occasionally, while I was forced to be mama 24/7.

Jamal will never admit it, but he was a deadbeat dad. He will never understand the problems I encountered – no man could ever understand. Mama's baby, papa's maybe isn't just a cliché – it's a fact. Make no mistake about it; I know a man's role is vital in the raising of a well-rounded child. But, women have proven and continue to prove that a mother's love is the closest thing to nirvana any of us will experience during our short stint on this earth.

Along with learning how difficult it is to be a mother, I learned a lot about people after Jada was born. At least once a week I would see some of my old "private school" girlfriends. The same people whom I'd once hung out with at the mall started to treat me like the scum of the earth.

My eyes were forever opened when one day I stood at the bus stop in the rain with a small umbrella covering Jada. I noticed a shiny red, Chevy Beretta at the red light. Sitting in the passenger seat of the car was Tanesha – the girl who accompanied me to the clinic the day I discovered I was pregnant with Jada.

"What's up girl," Tanesha yelled as she rolled the window halfway down trying to limit the amount of rain that got in the car.

"Nothing just trying to get my baby out of this rain," I responded, hoping that my old friend would catch the enormous hint I'd thrown at her and let me get in.

"Girl that baby is too cute. Call me when you get a chance," Tanesha yelled and then rolled up the window after the light turned green.

As if on cue, the rain started to come down harder as soon as the car drove away. I was stranded at a bus stop with no shelter. Only the massive raindrops splattering on my face could disguise my tears.

A few minutes later an older woman drove up to the red light. She looked over and saw me standing in the rain, and gestured for me to come over.

"Child get in this car and get outta that rain. You and that baby gonna get sick," demanded the lady with the authority of a seasoned grandmother.

I had never seen the lady before, but I was not about to turn down this offer. When I got inside the car the lady reached in the back seat and pulled a huge beach towel from a basket of clothes. The clothes smelled like they had been doused in fabric softener, making the old car smell incredibly fresh.

I dried Jada off as the kind old lady gave me a ride home. Not once did my baby cry. She seemed to be more at peace than me. Few words were spoken as the old lady hummed a gospel tune and focused on the road. I pointed to my apartment when she turned onto my block, and as I attempted to exit the car the lady reached over and grabbed my wrist and pulled me back in. She opened her huge purse, pulled out a fifty-dollar bill, and placed the money inside my trembling hand. I was stunned by this gesture. I didn't know this lady – probably would never see her again – and she was giving me money.

I started to cry and couldn't stop. I had just wiped the rain from my face, but now it was soaked again from my tears. I shook my head and said no, but my false pride couldn't hide my desire to take the money. The lady grabbed my wrist and forced the money into my hand and said, "Baby I was in your position years ago, and I made it. You just believe in GOD and he will see you through these rough times."

I thanked the woman and exited the vehicle. As I walked towards my front door I whispered in Jada's ear, "I'm sorry baby, but I promise you – this won't happen to us again."

I vowed from that point on that I would do whatever I needed to do to make sure my baby and I were taken care of. I didn't care about anything or anyone else. I'd made a vow to my child that I intended to keep.

Chapter 3 - *Let The Drama Begin*

Jamal

It was 1992, Jada was five years old, and my involvement in her life had been limited up to that point. It wasn't that I didn't love her, but I still hadn't fully embraced fatherhood.

After I graduated high school, my old girlfriend Dawn agreed to give our relationship another shot. We dated for a few years, and in 1992 I proposed to her. Dawn agreed to marry me, and life was great – until I got orders sending me to Asia. I was so bothered by my new assignment that I actually contemplated going AWOL. I hated the thought of leaving the United States, my family, my daughter, and most importantly my new fiancée.

Dawn's family took care of the wedding arrangements while I was in Asia; however, my absence during the planning process proved to be a bigger problem than I anticipated.

Dawn's father paid for the wedding, and her mom and aunts helped her plan all the details. I had to rely on long distance phone calls to get the scoop on how things were going. I constantly spoke to my mom and sister to make sure I had the names of everyone on my side of the family who wanted (and expected) to attend the festivities. I called Dawn weekly to convey my suggestions and wants. It was somewhat awkward at times, but all things considered - things went relatively smoothly...well, almost everything.

Dawn had a younger cousin who was five years old...approximately the same age as Jada. The child was beautiful and was ideal for the flower girl position...but so was Jada. Without discussing the flower girl situation with me, Dawn appointed her cousin to be the flower girl at our wedding. Whether she was pressured into this decision or it slipped her mind I wasn't sure, all I knew was that I had to clean up this colossal oversight fast. But, how do you conduct damage control from another continent?

Dawn and I hadn't even "jumped the broom" and we were already about to have our first bout of "baby mama drama." I was between a rock and a hard place. I needed guidance so I called my mom to get some of her infinite wisdom.

"Hello."

"Ma, I'm glad you answered the phone. I need your advice on how to deal with some drama that's about to go down."

"If it's involvin' Jada not being the flower girl at your wedding then sweetheart this is a call you should've made weeks ago."

"You mean Tracy already knows?"

"Well Jamal, the wedding is three weeks away, and no one ever contacted her about getting the child ready. It ain't hard to figure out that Jada isn't gonna be in the wedding."

"Shit! Shit! Shit!" I blurted out.

"Boy, watch your mouth!"

"I'm sorry mama, but you're gonna have to give me a pass on this one. Shit! How do I fix this? Mama, what should I do?"

My mom's response was not what I expected. She gave it to me straight – no chaser.

"To be honest with you baby I don't know what to tell you. Even if ya'll weren't gonna put Jada in the wedding you should have told Tracy that."

"Mama I didn't even make that decision. I'm way over here in Asia. Dawn and her family are making all of the arrangements."

"So you don't have any say? It's your wedding too!"

"Yeah I know, but honestly mama this one snuck up on me. I don't even think Dawn thought about it."

"Baby please! If you think this didn't cross Dawn's mind then you are being naive. Honey this is just the "tip of the iceberg" so you should start getting used to it."

"What do you mean?"

"Sweetheart look...Dawn is still young. She's obviously uncomfortable about introducing her new husband's five-year-old child to her entire family. So, she made the wedding plans with her family and totally ignored the issue. Meanwhile, Tracy is sittin' over there pissed because she thinks you're ashamed of her child...your child! She thinks you don't want Jada in your wedding."

"But mama I didn't..."

"Jamal it doesn't matter at this point. No woman wants her child to be ignored. Tracy thinks you're ashamed of Jada, and you know her instigating family is over there encouraging her."

"So what do I do?" I asked, expecting my mom to unleash some of her usually reliable advice.

"Get ready for the bullshit because you're about to have one pissed off "baby mama" on your hands. I will tell you this, whatever issues Dawn has with you havin' a child, she's gonna have to get over them because it's a package deal. When she gets married to you she is also marrying your child. I suggest you have a long talk with Dawn. You see Jay, this is a "woman" thing. As much as I hate to admit it, Tracy has a legitimate reason to be a little pissed behind this one."

I bid my mom farewell, hung up the phone, and started dialing Dawn's phone number. Before the long distance operator could connect the call I hung up the phone. I realized that I had no idea what I was gonna say to Dawn. I had all types of thoughts running through my mind:

Should I call Dawn and yell at her for putting me in this position? Was this an indication of how she and her family would try to control things once we got married? Should I be more understanding of Dawn's feelings, and calmly discuss the situation with her? Should I demand that Dawn make arrangements to let Jada be the flower girl? Should I demand that there be two flower girls? Should I call Tracy and ask for forgiveness?

I thought so hard about this dilemma that I started to get a headache. After stressing for a few more minutes I finally made a decision...I decided to go get drunk.

The next day I called Dawn and discussed my dilemma with her. Initially there was a little tension, but Dawn was more receptive to what I had to say than I thought she'd be. We both agreed that the damage had already been done, and to call Tracy three weeks before the wedding would only make matters worse. In the end, we agreed to be more open about our thoughts regarding the wedding arrangements, and any other issues we may have so that this type of confusion wouldn't happen again. As far as the Tracy situation, we both were prepared to deal with her wrath.

It was a good thing we braced ourselves for the oncoming storm too, because when it came, it came with the force of a hurricane. One week before the wedding, Tracy changed her home phone number and refused to give it to me.

Tracy

As beautiful as my child is, I couldn't believe that Jamal wouldn't put her in his wedding. To make things worse, he didn't even have the guts to call me. But, that's okay I dealt with his ass. I changed my phone number and I didn't let him see her.

It took me a few months to get over my anger, but by the summertime I reopened the lines of communication. I let him think that I re-established contact with him for Jada's sake, but the real reason was because I'd met a guy that summer who wanted me to take a trip with him to California. By this time, Jamal had returned from China, Korea or wherever he was overseas, and moved to Georgia. I needed a babysitter for Jada so I let her go visit Jamal and Dawn while I was gone to California.

Dawn seemed to accept Jada unconditionally. She treated Jada as if she was her own child. It was not uncommon for the two of them to leave Jamal behind while they went out and did "girlie" things. I was pleased that my daughter had a good relationship with Dawn. But, I knew it was just a matter of time before Dawn would want to have Jamal's baby. That's why the news that Dawn was pregnant didn't surprise me. Still, I had to call him and let him know I'd heard about the pregnancy and remind him of his priorities.

"So you're gonna be a daddy again? When were you gonna tell me?" I asked him. I remember that he got defensive.

"I didn't know I had to tell you; it ain't none of your damn business!"

Once I knew I had him upset I put the pressure on him, "Yeah it's my business. Especially if it's gonna affect you takin' care of Jada."

"Girl what in the hell are you talkin' about? Jada is well taken care of!"

"She's well taken care of now, but what's gonna happen when ya'll have that baby?"

"You know what? You're in grown folk business...stay in your place," he replied.

That fool told me to stay in my place! I had to check him. "Whatever! You just better remember my baby."

"Whatever!" he responded, having heard enough of my whining. "Where is Jada?" he asked.

"She's at my sister's house. Call her back later," I responded and then hung up the phone. I laughed because I knew that I had annoyed the shit out of him.

I learned quickly that image is everything. Armed with good looks and legs that seem to stretch for an eternity, I hit the New Orleans single scene with an attitude. At the age of 21, I had plenty of wanna be drug kingpins and "sugar daddy's" clamoring to be my sponsor.

Jamal always questioned my choice of companions, and had concerns about these men being around Jada. But there wasn't much he could do about it. I wasn't his wife – I was a single mother living on my own. I didn't give a damn if he got mad, he didn't ask for my blessing when he got married.

One day I called him to tell him some news that I knew would blow his mind.

"Hey Jamal, I just called to tell you that I'm getting married."

"Yeah right – who are you getting married to?"

"His name is Darwin."

"So when did you meet him?" he asked sarcastically.

"We've known each other for a few years. I just felt like you should know since Jada and I are going to move-in with him."

"Oh really! How well do you know this man? How do you know he can be trusted around Jada. I don't wanna have to come down there and fuck him up."

"Boy please! Darwin loves Jada like she was his daughter."

"Whatever! You just make sure that nigga knows that she ain't his daughter."

"Yeah, yeah...I just thought you should know."

When I hung up the phone, I laughed until my sides hurt. I'd won another round.

Jamal

Tracy and Darwin got married less than one month after she informed me of his existence. Miraculously, I saw a change in her attitude immediately. Darwin had a child from another relationship; it actually worked in my favor. Tracy spent the first six months of their marriage trying to impress him. It was the only time during Jada's life that I wasn't denied an opportunity to see her.

Don't get me wrong; there were some tense moments. Like the time I went to pick Jada up one weekend and had a run-in with Darwin.

I was in New Orleans for the weekend so I called one Saturday morning, and Tracy agreed to let me take Jada for the day. When I arrived at Tracy's apartment complex I wasn't impressed at all. At the entrance was a hooker ready to raise her dirty skirt up for anyone that had twenty dollars. The police were all over the place, and there were mattresses and garbage scattered around the overflowing dumpsters. The place wasn't as bad as some of the projects in New Orleans, but it wasn't that far removed. Tracy wasn't home when I got there, but her new husband was. That's when things got tense.

"Who is it?"

"This is Jamal – I came to get Jada."

Darwin came to the door holding Jada in his arms. At first I wondered why he was carrying a five-year-old child like she was an infant. The next thing I noticed was that he wasn't wearing a shirt and had on a pair of real small sprinter style shorts.

He was about four inches taller than me, and looked like he needed a shave. My first impression of him was that he looked like a big ass sissy wearing those shorts, but as I watched him holding my child I suddenly envisioned a pedophile standing before me.

"Tracy's not here and she didn't tell me you were coming to get Jada."

"I didn't come for Tracy, I came to pick up my daughter," I responded as I reached to take Jada from him.

"Well she didn't tell me you were coming," Darwin replied and took a step backwards to prevent me from grabbing Jada.

"What does that have to do with me? Man, give me my little girl," I replied, in a tone that clearly suggested I wasn't going to ask again.

"Look dog, I need to call her," said Darwin, looking extremely uncomfortable at the situation he found himself in. He had reason to feel uncomfortable because I was prepared to split his head.

After he released Jada to me he said once again, "I'ma give Tracy a call – she's at her girlfriend's house."

I looked Darwin in the face and said, "You can call her all you want – tell her I got Jada."

I could see that Darwin wanted to ask me to wait until he got Tracy on the phone. Fortunately for him he wisely kept his mouth shut. He'd never met me before so there was a natural hesitancy. However, I suspect that a portion of the fear in his eyes could have been attributed to thoughts of how Tracy would respond once she found out I took Jada. His only other option was to try to stop me – that wasn't going to happen.

Darwin quietly watched me as I walked away. One of Tracy's neighbors who'd been watching the entire exchange smiled as I walked by. She was a huge middle-aged black woman wearing a tattered housecoat. She stood in her doorway with a cigarette hanging out of the corner of her mouth.

"That's a beautiful child," she said as I walked by. "You did the right thing, that's your baby and he needs to respect that."

I smiled at the lady and winked my eye. Jada and I went to the park, and had a great time. Neither Tracy or Darwin mentioned the incident – I'd made my point.

It wasn't long before I learned that sometimes you have to make your point twice to baby mama and step daddy.

There's an old saying, *if you want to know the truth ask a child*. Never was this statement truer than a few months later when I was having a very innocent telephone discussion with Jada.

"Hey baby girl – how are you doing?"

"Fine!"

"Why didn't you call me? When we went to the park you told me that you were going to call me."

"I was with my daddy!"

"What do you mean, I'm here in Georgia."

"No not you, my other daddy."

"Your other daddy?"

"Jada put your mama on the phone," I insisted as a tension knot formed in my neck.

A few seconds later Tracy came to the phone.

"Hello."

"Tracy, what in the hell is Jada talkin' bout?"

"What are you talkin' bout?"

"I'm talkin' about her comment. She said she was with her other daddy. Who the hell is she talkin' bout?"

"Awh boy, she's talkin' about Darwin."

"Why is she callin' him daddy?"

"What's the big deal, he's her step daddy. She's a baby she doesn't know any better. Besides, she's here with him everyday so she just started calling him daddy."

"I don't give a damn! He's only been her step daddy for a few months. I'm her daddy! If I wasn't involved in her life I could understand, but I'm here – I don't appreciate that shit!"

Tracy didn't respond, she just held the phone and sighed loud enough to annoy me. I was about to continue my tirade, but before I could go into my second stanza – the phone hung up. I called back, but the line was busy.

I thought about Jada's remark the remainder of the night. I couldn't sleep well – I needed to get to the bottom of this.

My alarm clock sounded at 6:00 a.m. – it was 5:00 a.m. in New Orleans. I knew Tracy left to take Jada to the nursery and went to work at 8:00 a.m. I remembered Tracy mentioned that Darwin worked the night shift at his job; therefore, I knew that if I waited until it was approximately 9:00 a.m. I'd be able to catch him at home alone.

"Hello."

"Say Darwin, this is Jamal. I need to ask you somethin'."

"Yeah what's up?"

"My baby referred to you as her daddy. I wanna know why are you down there letting my child call you daddy?"

"Look here dog, I'ma be straight up with you. I never felt comfortable with that."

"So why did you let her call you daddy? You should've corrected her and explained the situation to her."

"Tracy came to me and asked me if I was ok with Jada callin' me daddy. I told her I wasn't. Look here dog, I have a son with another woman and I wouldn't want my son callin' some other man daddy. I tried to stop Jada, but Tracy told me it wasn't a big deal."

"Well I'ma tell you like a man. I don't want my child callin' someone else daddy."

"I can respect that."

"Good – if you can respect that than we shouldn't have any problems from here on."

I hung up the phone feeling vindicated. I never told Tracy that I called Darwin and I never heard Jada refer to Darwin as "daddy" again. Three months later, Tracy and Darwin were separated. They were divorced within one year.

When Jamal Jr. was born, Jada was seven years old. Our bond became stronger, but my relationship with Tracy was getting worse. This new baby was going to cause some tension between Tracy and me.

The most obvious conflict would be the money. I knew that I'd have to distribute my money evenly between the two kids. In many ways it was a no win situation; if I spent more money on my new baby than I spent on Jada, Tracy would accuse me of ignoring Jada. If I scrimped on the money I spent on Jamal Jr., Dawn would accuse me of favoritism. I felt like I was facing an 18 year prison sentence, and I would be forced to answer to two wardens...Tracy and Dawn.

It wasn't long before I had to start serving my prison sentence. Tracy became more and more demanding. I gave her cash every month and paid for Jada's daycare, but Tracy would constantly ask for more money. The holiday season prior to Jada's birthday marked the first of what would become a monthly argument about child support. Tracy wanted more money than usual and she wasn't shy about asking.

"Jamal I need $150 dollars."

"Tracy, I just gave you $300 two weeks ago. Why do you need more money?"

Tracy hated when I asked her to explain why she needed money.

"Jada needs some clothes," she responded.

In the early stages of Jada's life that response would have sufficed, but once I got married, Dawn insisted that I change my modus operandi.

"Well if she needs more clothes I'll take her to buy some clothes when I come home next month on Christmas leave."

"Fine!" Tracy yelled, and hung up the phone.

I didn't sweat it; Tracy always got angry and hung up when she didn't get her way. Besides, I knew that if I attempted to call back to argue she would just let the phone ring - that would only anger me.

Joining the military and spending some time in different cities enabled me to realize that there was a lot more to life than the 17th ward, Shrimp Po-boys, 190 Octane Daiquiris, and hanging out on the lake front. My exploration into the world outside of the "Big Easy" really opened my eyes. Make no mistake about it, I still loved New Orleans, but the city's lack of progress in anything other than partying became a turn off.

My views of my hometown always caused a problem between Tracy and I because like so many New Orleanians, she didn't view the city as stagnant. Our opposing views on life begin to affect the way we raised Jada. When it came to agreeing on what was best for Jada we were always on different pages. This was never more apparent than on Christmas Day in 1993. I was sitting in Tracy's living room trying to put together a dollhouse that I'd bought Jada.

"Jamal, why did you buy Jada so many black baby dolls?" Tracy asked.

In my opinion, that was the dumbest question Tracy had ever asked, and the look I gave her made my thoughts perfectly clear. The curt response I gave solidified my viewpoint on the topic.

"Because, the last time I checked Jada was black!"

"Well I think that's a shallow way of looking at the world. I want Jada to feel comfortable with all people." Tracy replied.

I couldn't contain my frustration with Tracy's questioning any longer.

"Tracy you can buy little white baby dolls, but don't expect me to."

"Jamal, why are you making such a big deal about a damn baby doll?"

"I'll buy Jada a white baby doll the day I see a little white girl walkin' down the street holdin' a little black baby doll. I ain't never seen no shit like that in my life. All the shopping I did this year, I never once saw white parents breaking their necks to buy their little blonde hair, blue eyed, white daughters any black baby dolls. You can't stand here, and look me in the face and honestly say that you've ever seen a white parent buy a black baby doll."

"Jamal it's not that serious!" Tracy said as she rolled her eyes and walked away.

"No, it wouldn't be to you...sell out!"

These types of spats between Tracy and I were commonplace. I tried hard to not argue in front of Jada, but sometimes I just couldn't help myself. Raising a child is hard work; its damn near impossible to instill a value system in a child when the parents disagree on nearly everything.

The primary purpose for visiting New Orleans on this occasion was to be with Jada for Christmas; however, before returning to Georgia there was still one more piece of unsettled business I had to take care of.

On Monday morning I planned to go to the Child Support Enforcement office to find out the exact amount of money I should be giving Tracy each month. Up until that point, Tracy and I had never had a formal child support agreement. I felt it was time we got something formal because I knew I had sent Tracy over $300 the previous month, and I didn't count more than three outfits in Jada's closet. I intended to put a stop to that by placing myself on child support. Whenever Tracy called I felt like I was getting "jacked", and there wasn't a damn thing I could do.

I had some fear that I would be forced to pay more than what I was already paying, but that was a chance I was willing to take.

I knew that formalizing the child support payments meant there were plenty of headaches awaiting me in the not so distant future; therefore, I was determined to have a little fun before I headed back to Uncle Sam's military.

It was the weekend and Club Whispers was going to be "da bomb!" I had been in town for five days, and I still hadn't hooked up with my homeboy Greg. I decided to head over to Greg's house, and catch up with that fool.

As I pulled up in front of Greg's front door I could here Jodeci's hit single, *Come and Talk To Me,* blasting and Greg doing his best K-Ci imitation..

"What's up dog!?"

"Damn dude, you sound like shit. You need to quit trying to sing, and keep workin' on tryin' to be a pimp." I replied, while squinting and trying to adjust my eyes to see through all of the weed smoke that was in the air.

"Man you know I got that pimp shit all figured out so don't worry about that. What's up? Are we goin' out tonight? I got this fly new outfit I wanna wear."

"Hell yeah we goin' out. You think I came all the way home just to look at the walls?" I responded excitedly.

"I just had to ask dog. You know you don't even holla at a brotha when you come home. Now you spend all your time visiting the in-laws and shit. I'm surprised Dawn gave your ass a two-hour break."

Greg and I spent the next hour or so just catching up. I listened to him brag about all of the new "booty" he'd conquered since we last spoke, but was shocked when he told me that one of his one-night stands was coming back to haunt him.

Apparently, a girl named Bianca whom Greg worked with down at City Hall had been throwing the "coochy" at Greg for months. According to him, he never hooked up with Bianca because he really wanted her friend Monique. Once Greg conquered Monique, she told Bianca how good the sex was and before Greg knew it, Bianca was coming at him even harder. According to Greg, he tried to fight it, but felt he had no choice but to satisfy Bianca's curiosity.

"Man, remember that girl Bianca I told you about the last time you were home? That freak says she's pregnant with my baby."

"Dog, you gotta be lying!?" I responded as I looked at Greg in disbelief.

Greg's expression suddenly turned serious as he begin to tell me what happened.

"I ain't lying. As a matter of fact, she already told me she ain't havin' an abortion. I told her I ain't ready for kids."

"Well playboy, it's too late for that now because you're gonna have a little mouth to feed."

"Whatever! If she has that baby she's gonna be taking care of it herself."

I was surprised to hear what my friend was saying. I took a swallow of my beer and then asked, "How you gonna dis' your own baby?"

"Man I told her I didn't want any kids. She knew how I felt before we hooked up, and she told me don't worry about it because she was on the pill."

"You should have still worn a rubber."

"Jay, I tried to put on a rubber, but her freaky ass pulled it off and said she liked it raw. What the hell am I supposed to do? I'm not gonna sit there with a rock hard dick, and argue with her about wearing a rubber."

"Well dog, ain't no getting away now, she even knows where you work."

"Man that don't mean shit to me! I'll quit my job before I let any woman stick me up for child support."

Greg's comments puzzled me. I wasn't sure if he was serious or if it was the weed talking.

"Dog it ain't that serious," I said.

"Like hell it ain't! Jay I'm gonna be honest with you, I don't even remember Bianca's last name. I know she told me, but I forgot it. All I know is that I had to "hit" that ass because it was callin' me."

"It was callin' you?" I was hesitant to ask, but I did anyway. "What was it saying?"

Greg took a long puff on his joint, smiled and replied, "That ass was saying - beat me up big daddy, beat me up!"

I couldn't help but chuckle. Greg had a way of telling a story and making facial expressions that would keep you laughing for days. He probably could have been a good comedian if he wanted to. Instead, he was about to be a daddy, and for the first time ever I could see fear in his eyes. Greg never had any real male role models. I knew exactly how he was feeling, because although my dad lived at home with us, my siblings and I all wished he didn't. Not having a decent male role model was the norm in our world.

Greg and I were both young black men who'd recently ventured into adulthood and were both equally lost. I didn't make any more comments because I could see that Greg was already stressing about the future and needed time to think. I also knew it would be hard for him to adjust his fast paced lifestyle around a child. Fatherhood would mean Greg would have to give up shopping sprees at the mall for himself, and use the money to buy clothes for the baby. He was about to find out what it meant to be somebody's "baby-daddy."

My visit to the Child Support Enforcement office was the first in what would prove to be several non-enjoyable trips. The women working inside the drab office building made every man feel like a "deadbeat" dad. Even non-employees walking by looked at me with disgust. It got to a point where I wanted to get on the intercom system and scream; *NO ONE IS MAKING ME PAY CHILD SUPPORT - I'M HERE BY CHOICE!*

"How much do you owe?" asked the middle-aged receptionist as I approached. Her words were condescending and dismissive. She didn't even bother to look up from her crossword puzzle.

"I don't owe anything, and y'all didn't make me come in here. I came up here on my own to discuss starting payments."

The woman stopped pretending to be interested in the crossword puzzle and looked at me with surprise. She maneuvered the piece of gum in her mouth and made it pop repeatedly. She rolled her eyes at me and then instructed me to sign in and have a seat. At no point did she apologize or express any embarrassment for assuming I was the typical "deadbeat" dad. She simply continued working on her crossword puzzle, and used the same condescending tone on the next guy that came in.

After what seemed like an hour-long wait, a caseworker finally came out into the waiting area and addressed me. She escorted me to her office, and asked why I'd come in. I told her that I felt Tracy was asking for too much money, and was not using the money on Jada. She asked me to state Tracy's full name and if possible her social security number. She started searching her computer files for a few seconds, and then gave a perplexed look before her next comment.

"Mr. Simms, it appears that Ms. Tracy Newhouse was just in here two months ago attempting to start child support payments."

"She never told me that. What happened?" I asked.

"Apparently, we gave her some paperwork to fill out, but she never came back. Since you are here we can go ahead and begin the process. Do you know that you are going to have to pay six years worth of back child support? Have you been paying child support for your daughter Jada?"

"Of course I've been taking care of my daughter!" I replied, and reached inside of my jacket and pulled out an envelope. "As a matter of fact, I have receipts and money orders from the past six years that prove I've been taking care of my child."

The caseworker took possession of my receipts and left the office. A few minutes later, she returned with an unidentified lady who was holding a folder. The second lady looked at me and asked, "Did you realize that for the past six years Ms. Newhouse has been receiving government assistance to take care of your daughter?" She took another glance at the folder and then continued, "By showing us these receipts you have now proven that Ms. Newhouse has been committing fraud. We can't pursue the case unless you file a complaint. Do you want to file a complaint?"

"What do you mean fraud? All I want to do is get a formal payment agreement so that I don't have to deal with Tracy extorting extra money from me!"

Both ladies seemed disappointed that I wasn't concerned about the fraud issue. Personally, I didn't care about Tracy getting money from the state. Truth be told, if I could have figured out a way to beat the system I would have done the same thing. All I wanted was to get my issue settled.

By the time we were finished making the child support arrangements, both caseworkers seemed to be on my side. I was instructed to pay $250 a month. I was fine with the judgment because up until that point I was already averaging closer to $300 a month in daycare expenses, clothes, and gifts. Both caseworkers admitted that it was refreshing to finally get a case where the man wasn't a "deadbeat" who drove an expensive car, wore expensive jewelry, but refused to pay child support.

My actions must have been out of the ordinary because one of the caseworkers became extremely talkative and generous. She walked over to the copy machine and started making copies of the document inside the folder. Much to my surprise, she then turned to me and gave me a copy of the original documentation filled out by Tracy. I graciously accepted the paperwork and got the hell out of there.

Despite the fact that Greg told me I was a fool for placing myself on child support, I was happy that things turned out the way they did. If I could just figure out a way to make my payments and stay out of that office I would be fine. The negativity and tension that surrounded that building was overwhelming.

The child support office was located on Canal Street. Parking was so scarce that I had to park two blocks away from the building. As I walked to the car I briefly looked through the 10-page document. Eventually, I came to a question and answer section that required Tracy to explain the circumstances surrounding her pregnancy. While reading that section, I would read a question and answer that would prove to haunt me for the rest of my life. The question read:

"Did you have sexual intercourse with anyone other than the alleged father of the child 30 days before or 30 days after the presumed time of conception?"

Tracy's answer was, *"Yes!"*

I've never had a heart attack, but I'd bet everything in my bank account that the pain resembles what I was feeling. My heartbeat changed - I could feel it flutter. It felt like birds were trapped inside of my upper torso flapping their wings. I was overwhelmed with a hurt and anger like nothing I'd ever felt, and for the first time in my life I felt like I wanted to hit a woman.

Up until that point all I had to go on were rumors about Tracy's promiscuity, but now I had proof that she'd been sleeping with someone else during the time we were together. What was even more disheartening was the reality that Jada may not be my daughter. What should I do? If I confronted Tracy she would simply deny everything. Knowing her, she would probably ban me from seeing Jada. If I asked for a blood test it would look like I was trying to avoid paying child support. Besides, I'd been told that once a man's name is placed on the birth certificate and he acknowledges paternity, he's on the hook for child support until the child turns 18 years old...period!

I was confused and really didn't know what to think or believe. I headed straight to Greg's house, and like a true "shade tree" psychiatrist, Greg tried to give me a little advice.

"Jay, I told you Tracy was scandalous. Man you need to go and get you a lawyer and try to get yourself out of this shit before it's too late."

"Greg, I can't afford a lawyer. Besides, my leave is up in two days. I just need some time to think."

"Well, I hate to say it, but I told you so," said Greg as he walked away shaking his head.

I decided to tell Tracy that night that I'd placed myself on child support. I contemplated letting her know about the document I had in my possession, but was afraid that if I told her about the incriminating document she wouldn't let me see Jada. Tracy had stopped me from seeing my child for various trivial reasons over the years; therefore, I knew she would go ballistic behind this.

Chapter 4- Playa, Playa

Jamal

Greg viewed all attractive women as prey that needed to be captured. Once he got a woman in his sights, he would swoop down on her like a vulture. Pretty soon, the woman would be helpless against his charm and good looks. Greg was not the type of brotha who was interested in settling down, and he let every woman he dealt with know that from the very beginning. His motto in life was: *no commitment, no stress.*

Now 24 years old, Greg still had no idea where his life was headed. After pretending to be interested in college for two semesters he decided to drop out so that he could pursue a career in acting. He moved to Los Angeles for five months, but couldn't get into show business because he spent more time chasing skirts than he did chasing roles. He was enamored with the fast pace and easy sex that came his way in Los Angeles. He used his southern accent and charm to attract and keep the attention of the California women (black, white, Asian, and Hispanic). However, it wasn't long before he became bored and moved back to New Orleans. It took awhile for him to readjust to the slower pace down south, but it wasn't long before he hit his stride.

Despite his fear of commitment, Greg always admired his friends who seemed to have found that one special woman to settle down with. Nevertheless, Greg was a firm believer that any man who got married before the age of 30 was a damn fool. Whenever he would begin to daydream of meeting "Ms. Right" and having a monogamous relationship, he would quickly snap out of it. The thought of sleeping with the same woman for years on end was sobering to him. Commitment simply was not Greg's cup of tea, and his actions proved that every other day.

In many ways, Greg's mom helped create his low opinion of women when he was young. She even encouraged his womanizing as he became older. Throughout his life she flaunted her handsome son around like he was some type of trophy. All of her friends would rave about his wavy hair and cute face. The more compliments thrown at him, the more his mom showed him off, and the more braggadocios she became. In many ways, Greg was destined to be vain and self-centered...it was all he had been taught. As he got older, Greg and his mom acted less and less like mother and son, and more like brother and sister.

After he graduated high school Greg's mom continued to perpetuate his sense of entitlement, and encouraged his vain behavior. She even began searching for partners for her son, and what better candidates than the young attractive flight attendants she worked with.

When Greg was 20 years old he accompanied his mom to her company's Christmas party. As the night came to an end she introduced him to three of the flight attendants she worked with. Each woman was drop dead gorgeous, and Greg was literally frothing at the mouth. True to form, within one month Greg started dating all three women. When they found out all hell broke loose. Initially, Greg's mom seemed to find her son's popularity with her coworkers amusing. As a matter of fact, she reveled in it the same way she did when he was younger. Her amusement ended when the bickering between the women turned into physical confrontations. Once the women realized that his mom had assisted her son in his manipulation of them, the tension became so intense that she contemplated quitting her job.

One evening after traveling back and forth from New Orleans to Chicago – Ms. Johnson's co-workers tried to talk her into going to a nearby bar to have drinks. She was somewhat interested, but she didn't like many of the women in the group. The torrential rain played a role in her decision to decline the invitation and head home.

She quickly made her way to her car in the employee parking lot and headed for Interstate 10 East. On her drive home she could barely keep her eyes opened. All she could think about as she swerved through traffic was her king sized bed.

Ten minutes into her drive Greg called her car phone and asked his mom to stop at the grocery store to pick up a gallon of milk. She didn't want to go to the store, but because her beloved son asked she went anyway. While in route to the grocery store Greg's mom fell asleep at the wheel, lost control of her car, and drove into a light pole. She was pronounced D.O.A at the hospital. When his mother hadn't made it home an hour after he spoke to her on the phone, Greg knew that something wasn't right. He called her car phone repeatedly but she never answered. Two hours later his suspicions were confirmed. The police contacted him and told him that his mom had fallen asleep at the wheel.

Greg's mom's death left a void in his life that he was incapable of dealing with. His dad abandoned him when he was five years old, and he was never real close with his extended family. Other than me, he trusted no one. Unfortunately, I lived in Georgia with my wife and new son, leaving Greg no one to turn to in his time of need. Rather than deal with his loss in a productive manner, Greg turned to what he knew best...sex. A man whose soul is empty will always turn towards his biggest vice for comfort, and that's exactly what Greg did. He slept with anyone who would give it up.

Greg and I talked on the phone often, but we could never seem to synchronize our schedules whenever I came to town. It had been two years since we last saw each other, and I was determined to see him during this trip.

As I pulled into the driveway at Greg's house, I was astonished at what I saw. The first thing I noticed as I pulled up was the brand new Jeep Grand Cherokee sitting in the driveway. I used the key Greg had left under the doormat to enter. Just like the exterior, the interior of his house had been totally remodeled. The entire bottom floor had beautiful hard wood floors. The kitchen had new appliances and counter tops. The living room was decorated with very stylish paintings and leather furniture.

Greg even had a picture of his daughter Mya on the fireplace mantle. I found this shocking because the child was two years old, and I hadn't heard Greg say much about her after her birth. I surveyed the

scene for a few minutes, and then got down to the
business at hand.

"What's up dog...how you doing?"

"Damn nigga – you don't know how to ring a
doorbell? You scared the shit out of me!"

"My bad dog, I didn't mean to make you nervous
and shit."

"Whatever, your ass damn near got shot," Greg
replied as he gave me some dap.

"So what's been up my brotha?"

"You know me baby I'm cool. How's that married
life treatin' you? You startin' to get fat, you'd better
stop sitting around the house playing scrabble and get
a life." Greg replied as he attempted to clean up
broken glass from inside the dishwasher.

"I got a life dog. You do enough ripping and
running for the both of us. Seriously dog, how are you
doing? I know you miss your mama."

"Yeah I miss her, but I can't change what
happened."

"Are you still seeing the psychiatrist to help you
get through this?" I asked.

"Nah dog, I had to stop going to her." Greg replied
as he walked into the living room and handed me a
beer.

"Why? What happened?"

"Man I caught her checkin' me out one day, so I
had to step to her. A few days later I had her faced
down and ass up right there on that sofa where you're
sittin'."

"What?" I asked, not believing what I was hearing.

"Yeah dog, I was hittin' it for about two months
and then from out of the blue she started tellin' me
she'd compromised her professional oath, and she
couldn't see me again."

"You sound like you don't believe her."

"Man I don't believe that. She wasn't worried
about her oath when she was ridin' this dick. I think

her ex-husband found out she was sexin' somebody and she got spooked."

"Man you'd better be careful, brothas are crazy these days."

"He can be crazy all he wants. He run over here and he's gonna be picking hollow points outta his ass. That fool had better check his woman!"

I took a long gulp of my beer and then started chuckling as Greg's confession sunk in.

"Damn dog, you fucked your shrink?"

"I had to get her dog, she was lonely. Shit, I went there to get help, and the next thing you know I'm counseling her."

"Sounds like you should've been charging her."

Greg looked at me and gave that same mischievous smile he'd often give back when we were in high school.

"I did charge her fool...you think I'm givin' these dick consultations away for free. Who do you think bought that television you're watchin'?"

Greg started to laugh, and as much as I wanted to play the, *I'm mature, I got my head on straight role*, I couldn't...so I laughed right along with him.

Greg's womanizing may have been wrong, but the stories behind his conquests were usually hilarious. Despite my disapproval of many of his tactics, in some ways I envied Greg's freedom. Every man goes through those moments when he wishes he wasn't married, and I wasn't any different. As much as I loved my wife, one of my guilty pleasures was to live vicariously through Greg. Often times I picked him for details just so I could laugh out loud as he described his encounters.

But, the one thing I could never condone was Greg's lack of participation in his daughter's life. Whenever the opportunity presented itself I would bring up Greg's daughter Mya.

"I see you got a picture of Mya up there. How old is she now? How is she doing?"

"She's almost 3 years old now, but to be honest with you dog I don't know how she's doing because I haven't seen her since we took that picture."

"What do you mean you don't know?"

"Just what I said fool, I don't know! I just keep that picture up there because it's a good conversation piece. Dog I'm tellin' you, once those freaks see you on a picture with your kid, it ain't gonna be long before they're lettin' you see them butt ass naked!"

"Dog, that's how you view your little girl...like a conversation piece to get some pussy? That's foul!"

"Whatever man, I told Bianca I didn't want a kid, but she had the baby anyway. At first I tried to play the daddy role, but I'm sorry, I can't fake it. That parenthood stuff ain't for me."

"Man that ain't right. You need..."

"Hold up dog. The only thing I need to do is stay black and fart to release gas," Greg blurted out – abruptly cutting my comments short. "You need to take that preaching somewhere else because I ain't tryin' to hear that. This ain't the Oprah Winfrey show."

I humbled myself and said, "For sho! You right dog, let's change the subject. But, that's still some dumb shit."

"And you can still suck on these." Greg replied.

"These what?" I asked curiously.

"These NUTS!!!" he blurted out as he grabbed his crotch.

As always, our disagreement ended in a good laugh. We had our own way of communicating to each other, and although we pretended not to listen - we always heard what the other had to say. We'd mastered the art of agreeing to disagree. We knew that our friendship was unconditional; therefore, we could say whatever needed to be said without reservation.

Greg and I changed clothes and hit the club. We pulled in front of the club like superstars, feeling good from all the beer we had been drinking. Greg was in rare form. Within twenty minutes he had already been given one phone number, and he was on the dance floor working on the second. I ordered a Heineken and chatted with people I hadn't seen in years.

After fumbling through a conversation with an old girlfriend who appeared to have gained 100 lbs., since I'd seen her last, I decided to take a stroll around the club. This was the first time that I had been in a club since I got married, and I wasn't sure how I should act. There were attractive women all over the place, and because my marital status prohibited me from saying anything too flirty – I felt awkward being there. I was 24 years old, but I felt as out of place as that 50-year-old man that seems to be present in every nightclub.

I started looking for Greg, but I was having a hard time trying to spot him amongst the sea of hair weave and fake gold chains. Eventually, I found a vacant spot on a wall. I sipped on my drink and watched all of the "eye candy" walking around the place. It wasn't long before I inadvertently made eye contact with a woman that could've given Halle Berry a run for her money. She was drinking what appeared to be a Tom Collins, and would occasionally glance my way as she talked to her friends.

A few seconds passed and she tried to look disinterested by turning away, but it was too late – I had already caught her checking me out. I stood there contemplating whether or not I should ask her to dance. She glanced again and saw that I was still staring. I too was trying not to be so obvious, but I couldn't help it – the girl was beautiful. There was definitely a connection.

Finally our eyes met and neither of us turned away. I gave her a nervous smile, and I could feel my knees shake when she smiled back. She started rocking and swaying in her seat and bobbing her head to the beat of a song that came on. It was obvious that she was trying to entice me to come over and ask her to dance. This wasn't good. This beautiful woman was giving me the green light to step to her, and I was leaning towards doing it.

As the base sound spewed from the huge speakers the crowd started moving towards the dance floor. Now there were no bodies blocking our view of each other. We were both blatantly undressing each other with our eyes. I stood there rubbing my wedding band with my thumb as I thought:

She wants to hook up. I could probably tap that ass tonight, but somebody might recognize me. I could take her to Greg's house, but damn - I'm married. I've never cheated on Dawn, but I've never had anyone this fine flirt with me. No one will ever know.

Eventually lust won out and I decided to go for it. Just as I was about to make a move I heard a man and woman arguing less than 10 feet from where I was standing. I tried to see what was going on, but I couldn't see clearly because of the people gathering around. One bystander finally moved and I could see that the arguing couple was Greg and Bianca. I was unsure of what the problem was, but their conversation seemed to be getting pretty intense. Before things got worse I decided to intervene.

"What's up with you two? Ya'll are makin' a scene in here."

Greg's fists were clinched and he looked as though he was about to hit Bianca.

"Man I don't give a fuck! She walked up on me like she's lost her damn mind."

"I just said what's up. Your deadbeat ass just got mad because I told you your daughter has been askin' about you." Bianca yelled as she wiped the tears from her face.

"Don't flip the shit now, that's not how you approached me." Greg yelled back.

I'd heard enough, "Look, there's a time and a place for everything and right about now, ya'll looking pretty damn stupid standin' here arguing."

Bianca looked at me and rolled her eyes. She was about to say something else to Greg, but before she could get her words out I grabbed him by the arm and Bianca's friend grabbed her. I took Greg to the other side of the club, and bought him a drink. The mood was tense for a few minutes, but eventually his temper subsided and he started to relax.

The more relaxed he became the more he drank. It wasn't long before Greg was drunk, and in true drunken fashion, he got on his soapbox about women.

"Man I told that girl I didn't want a child, but she went ahead and had the baby anyway. Now she's mad at me because I don't come around. These women are a trip. On one hand they want you to be straight up with them, but when you come at them straight up they can't handle it. She must have thought I was gonna change my mind or something once the baby got here. I told her I wasn't ready to be a daddy. Every time you turn around one of these freaks tryin' to give a nigga a charge."

"Who else is trying to give you a charge?" I asked.

"Dog, I don't even want to talk about it. It's just more drama, and I don't feel like dealin' with it. Lets just say this - these women are scandalous. That's why I treat them the way I do."

Greg spent the next two hours talking to every good-looking woman that passed by. Right before we left the club he was whispering in the ear of a woman that looked like she weighed 300 lbs. I saw that as a clear sign that Greg was stinking drunk, and it was time to go.

The two of us staggered and yelled good-bye to the few people we knew that were left in the club. As we walked across the parking lot I saw the beautiful Halle Berry look alike leaving the club...with a man who had his hand firmly planted on her ass. I guess I wasn't the only one she "connected" with.

Despite the unfortunate altercation with Bianca, we had a great time that night. Greg wanted to ride around the city in search of a new club, but I talked him out of it. If we had driven to any place other than Greg's apartment, which was five miles away, a DWI would've been the next incident.

As we pulled up to Greg's apartment we saw a woman standing in the driveway...it was Bianca. I was too tired to break up any more arguments so I left Greg and Bianca outside talking and went upstairs to the guest bedroom.

I pulled back the covers on the queen size guest bed and jumped in – still wearing my clothes. Within 15 minutes I was asleep.

The next day when I awakened I had a headache that was so excruciating it made my eyes water. I staggered out of the bedroom and headed towards the bathroom. I passed by Greg's bedroom, and noticed that the door was slightly open - so I peeked in.

Greg and Bianca were sprawled across the bed sound asleep...butt ass naked. I wasn't surprised; I knew Bianca wanted to get "worked over" when I saw her standing in Greg's driveway. The only reason a woman would go to a man's house at four o'clock in the morning is for sex. I just shook my head, chuckled, and closed the door. But, before I walked away I did take another peek inside the room...I never realized Bianca was that fine.

As I sat at the kitchen table eating a bowl of cereal I kept replaying the events of the night before over and over in my head.

As much as I disliked Greg's views on being a dad, I had nothing but respect for his honesty. It takes courage to be honest even at the risk of being criticized, and Greg was the most brutally honest person I knew. Greg told women up front what he would and would not do...take it or leave it. Ninety percent of the time the women willingly went along with his program. Was it his "pretty boy" looks? Was it his flashy lifestyle? Were the women he dealt with just downright desperate? I simply could not understand how a woman as attractive as Bianca could allow herself to get pregnant by a man who made it clear that he viewed their relationship as nothing more than a good "screw."

I tried to empathize with Bianca, but the more I thought about it, the more I viewed her as stupid. While sitting at the table staring at a black dot in my milk trying to determine whether or not it had legs, I begin to think about my daughter. Jada was a beautiful child, and one day she would have to deal with guys like Greg and their shady behavior. I was determined to do all I could to keep my daughter from making some of the same dumb decisions I'd seen other women make.

I glanced over at the picture of Mya on the wall. The picture made me think of a talk show I'd recently seen. The subject of the show was "Deadbeat Dads." One of the guests was a 24-year-old woman with four children (ages: 7, 5, 3, and 2) - all fathered by the same "Deadbeat Dad." The man had never provided financial support for any of his children, and when he came onto the stage the audience booed him. People were yelling at him, and one man in the audience even threatened to come on stage to fight him. I remembered being intrigued by the reaction of the audience. I noticed that the audience was ready to lynch the deadbeat dad, but no one said anything to the woman who allowed herself to be in that position. I recalled thinking to myself:

Someone needs to slap the shit out of her for continuing to have children with this man.

Finally, one audience member asked the girl why she kept sleeping with the man.

"Because he is real good in bed, and we make pretty babies together," the girl replied.

The audience went crazy, and turned on the girl. I thought the girl's response was ignorant, but I felt she was being honest. The truth is – there are some superficial women out there. The fact that Bianca waited outside of Greg's house at four o'clock in the morning was proof that some women are more than willing to tolerate being mistreated and disrespected by a man...especially if he has wavy hair and can "lay the pipe." There are women who enjoy "trophies" just as much as men.

Greg came into the kitchen wearing a robe but no underwear. My pensive moment was over at the site of Greg's dick swinging from side to side.

"Damn King Kong, maybe you should put on some drawers before you come swinging that thing in here."

"Don't get scared, I got this Anaconda trained."

We both chuckled as Greg poured some cereal into a bowl.

"Man I tell you what, that girl will wear you out. You should go get you some."

"Man get outta here with that," I replied.

"Boy you under estimate my skills. I'll betcha $50 I can hook that up for you," Greg said with a mischievous look on his face.

I tried to pretend like I was blowing Greg off. I tried not to look him in the face because he would have known I was interested. I wanted to get some more cereal, but I couldn't stand up because my penis was hard from the thought of having sex with Bianca. The only way to get out of this moral dilemma was to go on the offensive.

"What I look like takin' sloppy seconds? You think I want to put my dick somewhere your dirty ass has been?"

"Whatever! You don't want to go after me because you might fall in and never get out. Then I'd have to explain to Dawn how her man drowned in some other woman's pussy."

We both laughed again, and then started discussing our plans for the day. I told Greg that I was gonna go to Tracy's house to get Jada, but I needed to get some transportation. I asked Greg to drop me off at Tracy's house later on.

"At what time? I already told Bianca she could bring Mya over here today."

"What?!"

"Man you know how it is when you knee deep in those guts. She started cryin' and gettin' emotional so I felt obligated to say somethin' to shut her ass up." Greg paused for a moment as he stared at the milk in his bowl. "It was worth it because the minute I told her she could bring Mya over here she told me I could do whatever I wanted to."

"Oh yeah?" I asked, as my curiosity grew. By then I was so turned on by Greg's tale I started giving serious thought to his offer. Greg knew that he had my attention so he told everything.

"Fool did I stutter...I said "whatever." She grabbed me by my neck and told me I could have that booty. Dog, I damn near pulled a hamstring trying to run and get the KY jelly out of the closet."

At that moment, Greg's story was interrupted by Bianca's seductive voice calling from the bedroom.

"Greg come here," she purred.

"You hear that shit fool? That's called the, *I need some more of that dick purr!*" Greg said enthusiastically. "You wouldn't know anything bout that because the only thing your woman want to do after ya'll have sex is talk about politics and global warming. You need to get down on your knees and bow down before me fool."

I just sat there and shook my head. I was too horny to think about eating food – besides my corn flakes had turned soggy.

"So you're just gonna sit here all day? You ain't gonna take the child anywhere?" I asked.

"She's lucky I'm doing this," Greg replied. "I told her that she had one of two options: I can send her some money for the child, but I told her if I did that I wasn't gonna have anything to do with Mya."

"What was the second option?"

"The second option was that I'd spend some time with Mya, but if I did, I wasn't giving her any child support money."

"You gotta be shittin' me? You really told that woman that?"

"You damn right!"

"What did she say?"

"I just said Mya was coming over here later, so what do you think she said!?" Greg said with a chuckle as he placed his cereal bowl in the sink. "Look, I'm about to go tattoo that ass some more. Are you sure you don't want some?"

"Nah, dog – I'll pass," I replied, still trying to fully grasp the ultimatum Greg had given to Bianca. That was some of the coldest shit I'd ever heard him say.

"You can use my truck today if you want to - just make sure you bring it back with some gas in it."

I liked the idea of riding in Greg's new truck, but I was somewhat hesitant to let Tracy see me in anything that looked too expensive. I had absolutely no trust in Tracy. Experience had taught me that she would use anything she could think of to try to justify increasing my child support payments. If Tracy thought I could afford to buy a brand new SUV she'd be at the child support office the next day. Greg instinctively knew what I was thinking.

"Man, take the truck! I know what you're thinking. You sittin' here worrying about what Tracy's gonna think. If she asks something about the truck you tell her to mind her damn business," he barked.

"Man, I wish it was that easy." I replied.

"You see that's why I ain't volunteering to pay shit! That child support system got you scared to buy nice things for yourself. You spend all of your time worried about having to pay more child support. Meanwhile, these trifling ass women can take your child support check and spend it on anything. Whether it's their broke ass boyfriends or outfits for concerts – they don't have to account for a dime. They can spend your money on anything they want to, and the child might not see a dime of that money. But, you can't spend money on yourself without being audited."

Bianca called Greg a second time, causing him to lose track of his thoughts. Greg's attention switched quicker than a child with ADHD. Suddenly, the only thing he could think about was round two. He looked at me.

"This is the last time I'm gonna ask you, do you wanna get a piece of this ass or what? I'm tellin' you Jay, she's *bout it!*"

"Nah dog you go ahead and handle your business. Just remember all the stuff I taught you."

"Whatever! I should be teaching classes on how to lay the pipe."

Greg stood up and straightened his robe like he was a doctor going in to see a patient.

"Hold up girl I'm coming!" he yelled.

Greg looked back at me one last time, and gestured for me to come into the room. I thought long and hard (literally) about going into that bedroom and getting some sloppy seconds. Reluctantly, I gestured for Greg to go ahead without me. Greg shrugged his shoulders, and proceeded into the room to handle his business with Bianca.

Meanwhile, I sat at the table a little longer, and thought about Greg's comments. Once again I found myself torn. I didn't agree with Greg's stance on child support, but there was a part of me that agreed with Greg's opinion that the "system" was totally screwed up.

I sat there and thought a little longer until I heard Bianca moan. After I heard the second moan my hormones got the best of me. I tiptoed over to Greg's bedroom door and placed my left ear against the door so that I could listen to them have sex.

When my face pressed against the door it started to open. The door made a squeaky sound that startled me. I wanted to run away, but my penis kept telling me to take a peak.

Fuck it! I thought to myself as I opened the door to get a better view. What I saw was more than an eyeful. Bianca had her face buried down into the pillows and her pretty caramel butt up in the air. Greg was "hitting it from the back" while looking at me and smiling. Bianca raised her head up from the pillow and glanced at me. It was obvious she was a little embarrassed... just a little. She squirmed for a second as she tried to hide her exposed body under the covers, but Greg had a lock on her like a pit bull.

Greg gestured for me to come in, and I was surprised to see that Bianca didn't protest. She looked over at me and smirked when she saw that my penis was protruding out like a pole.

"Jay come get some of this - you know you want to," Greg blurted out, seemingly unconcerned about Bianca's reaction.

As Greg offered the mother of his child up on a platter, she let out a moan that clearly indicated she was climaxing – hard! It was almost as if Greg's generous offer turned her on.

At a glance, Bianca appeared to be extremely "high maintenance." She looked like the type of woman who would avoid sex for fear that the perspiration might ruin her makeup. But, behind closed doors she was obviously down for the "ménage a trois." As if on cue, she looked back at Greg and yelled, "Give it to me harder!"

I couldn't believe what I was witnessing. Bianca was clearly giving me an invitation to join in. I moved even closer to the edge of the bed, and pulled my penis out as Bianca stared and licked her lips like she was about to devour my manhood. My toes started to curl and my palms became sweaty as I anticipated getting the blowjob of my life.

My conscious took on the form of these two categories you see in the movies. The angel dressed in white appeared to be standing on my left shoulder telling me to walk away. I would have listened to this voice telling me that partaking in this threesome would ruin my marriage, but the angel's words were falling on deaf ears. Not because of wax, but because of the more persuasive argument from the devil on my right shoulder. The devil that kept telling me that Dawn would never find out.

Bianca made my decision a little easier. She grabbed my penis and pulled it towards her mouth. I could envision the little devil on my shoulder smiling. But, GOD has a way of saving us from our own ignorance. Just as Bianca was about to rap her voluptuous lips around the tip of my penis I heard my pager ringing in the other bedroom. I looked at the door, and then back at Bianca. I knew that it could only be Dawn calling me that time of morning. I was frozen with guilt.

Within a matter of seconds my penis went from being hard enough to cut diamonds to limp as a wet noodle. Like a teenager caught masturbating to a magazine, I was overcome with embarrassment. I pulled up my pants and scurried towards the bedroom door. As I left out I could hear Greg laughing and saying, "Jay come back dog, this pussy don't bite!"

After taking a nice cold shower, I put on a pair of comfortable Girbaud jeans and shirt, my brand new pair of white Reebok classics, and grabbed Greg's car keys. I took the car to a nearby detail shop to have it washed, and even had the interior cleaned to try and remove the stench of liquor and weed from the upholstery. Within thirty minutes the car looked and smelled brand new.

I proceeded to making the routine stops by various family members and friends scattered around the city. My goal was to see as many people as I could, in the shortest amount of time possible. But, before I could see any friends or family members I had to make one very important stop first – to see my mother.

I was extremely anxious to see my mom because she was now living on her own. After years of tolerating my dad's physical and emotional abuse, she'd finally built up the courage to leave. When I heard the news of their separation my respect for my mom reached a new plateau.

Our breakfast was beautiful. I took her to a nice black owned bistro located in downtown New Orleans one block away from Canal St. I ordered a steak and egg dish while she nibbled on an order of beignets. She tried to get me to indulge, but unlike most New Orleanians – I hate beignets. The powdered sugar residue sprinkled on the delicacy makes them more trouble than they're worth. Every time I eat one I usually get more powder on my face than in my mouth. To avoid the mess I simply avoid this New Orleans specialty like the plague.

We ate our breakfast and talked like a young couple on their first date. My mother spoke with an exuberance that I'd never seen before. She'd been liberated. I was witnessing the epitome of emancipation and it was an awesome site. As we completed our meals with a cup of hot coffee, she took off her "friend cap" and put on her "mama cap." As always, she could sense when I had something on my mind, and she knew how to get the truth out of me.

"Greg's car is real nice...how is he doing?" she asked as she sipped her coffee.

"He's fine...still crazy." I replied as I stared aimlessly at my cappuccino.

"You tell Greg that I said leave those fast ass women alone, and find someone to settle down with. These little hoochies got all kinds of diseases these days."

"You know Greg gonna do what he wants to do." I responded with a sly smile as images of Greg urging me to come join in his sexcapades flashed across my mind.

"Whatever little dirty thoughts you're thinking – get'em outta your mind – you're a married man now. You just tell him what I said, and tell him I said come see me."

"Yes mama!" I replied as I whirled the spoon around in the white foam that covered the top of the drink.

Still sensing that something was wrong, she decided to dig a little deeper.

"So, what are your plans today?"

"I'm gonna try to holla at a few people this morning. I'm supposed to pick up Jada at three o'clock this afternoon and take her to the movies."

"How is Jada? Tracy moved again and never bothered to give me the phone number so I haven't talked to my grandchild in weeks."

"Yeah I know. I'm gonna talk to her about that today when I go and pick up Jada."

My mother knew that Tracy and I had difficulty discussing issues so she attempted to downplay her comments with the hopes that it would defuse a possible argument when I met with Tracy later on.

"Jay, don't get caught up in that drama. You're only in town for one day. Just go and get your child, spend some quality time with her, and leave her crazy ass mama alone. You need to focus on that child and stop lettin' that girl get under your skin."

"Yeah I know, but she does some stupid stuff. You know why she changed her address and phone number?"

"No. Why?"

I pushed my cappuccino away and placed my elbows on the table and leaned forward so that my mom could hear what I was saying.

"She changed her phone number and address because I asked her to tell me how she was spending my child support money. We got into a big argument and then she hung up the phone in my face. I tried to call a few days later, and the phone number was disconnected."

My mother shook her head. She'd warned me that Tracy would present a problem – she called it "mama's intuition."

"Yeah I do remember you mentioning something about that. You never did tell me how you found her," she replied.

"I didn't have to look for her because she called me," I said, as I unsuccessfully tried to hide my annoyance. "Supposedly, Jada needed some new uniforms for school and Tracy didn't have the money.

So I made her give me her new phone number before I would send her the money."

My mother hated to see me mistreated, but she also knew that she needed to keep her emotions in check so that she could calm me down when I got like this. She reached across the table and grabbed my hand.

"GOD knows what you are going through, and he is going to bless you for doing the right thing...just hang in there. She may be getting the upper hand now, but in the end you are going to be the one who gets the blessing. Jamal, GOD see's everything - trust me, her day is coming."

Chapter 5 - *Deadbeat 101*

Jamal

Jada and I spent the day together and then I returned to Greg's apartment. When I arrived, I saw him stretched out on the sofa with one arm behind his head and the other hand lodged comfortably inside his boxer drawers. The fresh smell of popcorn resonated in the air.

"Nigga stop playin' with ya self! Did Mya come over?" I yelled from the kitchen.

"Nah, Bianca called and said she was going to bring her over here tomorrow evening. That's fine with me because I'm tired," Greg responded in a very monotone voice.

We gulped down a few beers and then went to sleep. I had so much on my mind that I could feel a headache coming on. I could feel it was going to be worse than the one I had earlier that morning. I said a prayer, closed my eyes, and went to sleep. But, it wasn't long before Greg interrupted me.

I jumped up - my heart was pounding feverishly. I couldn't quite focus in the dark bedroom. I looked over at the numbers illuminating from the alarm clock. It was 3:27 a.m., and I could hear yelling and cursing. At first I thought I was dreaming, but once I'd gathered my senses I realized that the cursing I heard was coming from Greg's bedroom. My first reaction was to go to Greg's room and check on my friend, but something told me to stop and listen. I opened my bedroom door slightly, and listened to Greg's phone conversation. I could only hear Greg's responses, but it was obvious that whomever he was talking to had pissed him off:

"Why do you keep callin' me with this?."

PAUSE

"I suggest you keep doing what you're doin' because I ain't givin' you a damn thing. I told you I wasn't going to take care of that child. I suggest you figure it out."

PAUSE

"That's your problem not mine. I ain't givin' you shit."

Greg slammed the phone down, and then put on his robe. I assumed he was moving towards his bedroom door so I moved away. Just as Greg opened his door to exit, I closed my bedroom door.

My alarm clock was set to ring at 4:00 a.m. so I decided to lay down for the remaining twenty-five minutes. As I lay in the bed staring at the ceiling I thought about Greg's reluctance to take care of his children. I didn't know who Greg was talking to on the phone, but it was obvious to me that it was someone other than Bianca. He'd obviously impregnated another woman and refused to take responsibility for the child.

I wondered how I could remain close friends with a guy who refused to take care of his children. I felt that Greg's attitude was a reflection on me some how. After all, birds of a feather flock together.

I found myself losing respect for my best friend. As much as I wanted to mind my own business and deal with my own problems, I couldn't help but view Greg with disgust. I took fatherhood seriously, and I wasn't sure if I could continue to hang out with someone who cared so little about being a dad.

As we drove to the airport, I couldn't resist asking Greg about the phone conversation I'd overheard. I knew it was none of my business, but we were best friends – nothing was off limits.

"Man I thought you and Bianca were doing okay. I heard you yellin' at her on the phone this morning," I said, trying to bait him into talking about it.

"My bad dog, I didn't mean to wake you up," Greg replied.

"No problem playa, I had to get up anyway."

"I didn't think you would wake up in time to catch this flight."

"Yeah I had my alarm set for 4 o'clock, but I didn't need an alarm clock because I heard you yelling. What are ya'll arguing about now?"

"Nothing important," Greg replied as he looked away.

"So, is she still buggin' you about taking care of the baby?" I asked.

"Actually, that wasn't Bianca; just another freak tryin' to force-feed a baby on me. I told her to let her current boyfriend take care of it."

"So you know it's your baby, and you're gonna let some other dude take care of your child?" I asked as I shook my head.

Greg was in no mood to be queried. He glanced over and saw me shaking my head - suddenly he became defensive.

"Why are you shakin' your head? Man don't start that preaching shit this early in the mornin'!"

"I ain't sayin' a thing!"

"You don't have to say anything, it's written all over your face."

"Nah dog, ain't shit written on my face – that's your conscious messin' with you."

"Man shut up! Just mind your business, and let me handle mine."

The tension in the car was so thick that it could be cut with a knife. Every friendship has a judgment day; a day when one or both parties find themselves reflecting on the friendship and trying to identify the tie that binds.

The unusual silence between the two of us was an indication that our views about life had changed. The entire weekend seemed to signal a difference in our maturity levels. For the first time in our lives it became apparent to both of us that our relationship had changed.

As Greg pulled up to the departure ramp at the New Orleans Airport, he couldn't hide his contempt for me. He felt as though I had taken several jabs at his lifestyle during that weekend. He felt that I'd spent far too much time passing judgment on him and his relationship with his child. For the first time in his life he was actually eager for me to leave.

As I retrieved my luggage from the back of the truck I turned around expecting Greg to be standing near offering a handshake and embrace. Much to my surprise Greg was still sitting in the driver's seat. I could see him staring at me through the rearview mirror. As I walked around to the curve I looked through the passenger side window and attempted to say goodbye.

"Thanks for the ride dog. Take care of yourself and stay out of trouble."

My statement wasn't any different from any other time I exited Greg's company. I didn't mean anything negative by saying, "stay outta trouble." To me this was just a figure of speech, but apparently Greg didn't take it that way.

"What you mean...stay outta trouble?" Greg shouted.

"Damn dog, what's wrong with you? I didn't mean anything," I responded, as I stood there somewhat stunned by Greg's mood swing.

"Bullshit! You meant something. You've been making your little slick ass comments about me the entire weekend. What are you trying to say? You think you're better than me now? You got married and now your shit don't stink?"

I was caught totally off guard by this outburst. I moved my bags away from the curb.

"Where the hell did that come from? What are you talking about?"

Before I could back away from the car Greg had thrown the car in park, exited the vehicle, and was walking towards me. Not knowing what he was thinking I instinctively dropped my bags and got ready to scrap. I didn't really want to fight Greg, but friend or not, I wasn't going to stand there and let him knock me out.

We were face-to-face and staring each other right in the eyes. Airport security came over and asked if everything was okay, but neither of us acknowledged the officer as we waited for the other to make a move.

Finally, I reached down and grabbed my luggage.

"Man I don't know what's wrong with you, but you'd better check yourself cause you actin' like a little bitch."

"No nigga you the one getting' played like a little bitch. Just because your ass getting screwed for child support you want me to be in the same boat."

I spent the entire 1½-hour flight back to Georgia thinking about the entire weekend - in particular, my argument with Greg. My thoughts were racing:

Damn, Greg's attitude change came from out of nowhere. Why was he tripping? Was I really being judgmental this weekend? Was I being condescending? Hell no I wasn't being condescending...he's foul and he knows it. His conscious is starting to mess with him, and rather than deal with his actions he wants to lash out at me. Well, maybe I was riding him a little too hard about his child. So he views me as some type of sucka because I take care of Jada? Fuck it; if he doesn't call me I'm not calling him.

Greg

I was highly pissed after I dropped Jamal off at the airport. That nigga is always tryin' to pass judgment on me. For years, I've had to deal with feelings of inadequacy when in his presence. I guess all that stuff that I had been keeping inside finally came out.

I really believed that Jamal harped on the child support thing because that's the only facet of his life where he had the upper hand on me. Of course, he'd never admit it, but I believe that deep down Jamal envied my lifestyle.

I went back to my house to change clothes and get ready for work. When I arrived there was a message on my answering machine from Bianca:

"Greg, I was just calling to see if you still wanted me to bring Mya over this evening. Call me and let me know what time is best."

I immediately started to regret having sex with Bianca the day before. I knew that the moment I "hit it" she would use that as an excuse to try to bring the kid around. I remembered agreeing to let Mya come over, but as far as I was concerned, once I climaxed all agreements were voided. I knew that was a foul way to handle Bianca and my child, but I decided to ignore the message and off to work I went.

After work I drove uptown to Club Tipitinas to catch one of my favorite jazz acts perform. I listened as the artist played his own rendition of songs from the Miles Davis classic album, *Kind of Blue*. While listening to the trumpeters' rendition of my favorite Miles Davis tune, *Blue and Green*, I noticed an old female acquaintance named Lisa leaving the club. I waved and gestured for her to come over.

Lisa was your typical New Orleans 7th Ward beauty. Her skin was golden brown and her hair was silky black and as wavy as the Pacific Ocean. From a distance she looked Hispanic – but the booty was too curvaceous to belong to anyone other than a sista. In modern vernacular she might be referred to as "yella", or even "redbone" – but being a native of New Orleans she naturally inherited the characterization of "Creole." Regardless of what term was used to classify her, the woman's beauty was undeniable.

Lisa stood approximately 5'7", 135 lbs., with an hourglass figure, flawless skin, and a smile that could stop a train. By watching this woman's swagger a blind man could see that a brotha would have to meet several requirements on her checklist in order for her to say hello.

On the downside – Lisa was the incarnation of the term "black bourgeois." For a brotha to even be allowed to buy her drink he had to earn a minimum of $60,000 a year or better (or at least give her the impression that he earned that much); he must drive a car that cost more than $40,000 (or at least have access to a friends car that cost that much); he must be a graduate of one of the local all male Catholic high schools (if he barely graduated it didn't matter - as long as he had a diploma); and he must be able to pass the "brown paper bag" test...an absolute requirement!

"What's up Greg? I haven't seen you in awhile. Where have you been?"

"I've been around. Damn girl, you're looking better every time I see you. Who are you here with?"

"I was supposed to meet my girlfriend here, but I got tired of waiting for her so I was about to leave."

Lisa and I spent the next hour drinking and becoming reacquainted. Shortly thereafter we left together and headed to my house.

We arrived at my apartment at 7:30 p.m., and by 7:45 p.m. we were screwing like rabbits.

It didn't take long for me to remember why I liked Lisa...she was a freak! She was more than ready to give it to me any way I wanted it.

Lisa was in the middle of giving me the mother of all blowjobs when the doorbell rang. My toes started to curl and my eyes rolled towards the back of my head, as I ignored the doorbell. Lisa looked at me and gave a sly grin – she knew I was about to blow. She slowly slid her tongue around the tip of my penis and then along the sides – the girl had skills. Without further ado, she went for the gusto...she licked my balls. My

butt cheeks puckered and I lost control. Sperm flew
everywhere as I screamed, "Oh shit!"

I grabbed her hair and started squirming like a
punk, but Lisa would not unwrap her lips from
around my balls.

Much to my vexation, the person on my doorstep
wouldn't leave. The ringing persisted. I reluctantly put
on a robe, and went downstairs to answer the door. As
I approached the front door I could see the silhouette
of a small child through the stained glass window.
Suddenly, I remembered that Bianca said she'd bring
Mya over. I was faced with a dilemma - should I open
the door and deal with Bianca and my daughter whom
I hadn't seen in two years or should I go back upstairs
and finish getting worked over?

Many men would have been paralyzed by the
feelings of indecisiveness and guilt as they attempted
to analyze this situation. But, for me it really wasn't
that hard of a decision. I never told Bianca what time
to bring Mya over; she should have waited until she
talked to me.

Chapter 6 - *Come And Get Her*

Jamal

Not much had changed by 1998. Jada was 11 years old, and I had come to grips with the fact that I was nothing more than a wallet. Tracy made it clear that my opinions regarding Jada's upbringing carried very little weight. The only time Tracy welcomed my opinion on an issue was when it didn't differ from hers. This frustrated the hell out of me because it seemed like the only time Tracy gave a damn about what I felt was when she needed me to pay for something she couldn't afford.

I took a leave of absence and drove to New Orleans to attend a parental conference with Jada's teacher. I actually arrived at the classroom before Tracy and the teacher did. I smiled proudly as I stood in the classroom amongst the miniature furniture waiting for everyone to arrive. I looked around to make sure no one was looking, and then I tried to sit at one of the desks. It was so small that my legs got stuck. I wrestled my way out of the chair and then started looking at the decorations on the wall. I noticed graded book reports displayed – Jada's report wasn't one of them. My mood changed as I remembered why we had been summoned – Jada wasn't performing well in school.

Tracy and the teacher walked into the classroom together. They were laughing as if they'd already had a meeting. The teacher introduced herself, and proceeded to tell me how Jada had been struggling, and would benefit from a smaller classroom environment.

I sat through the twenty minute meeting with the teacher wishing that the teacher would make her points and shut up. I felt that she was patronizing me – I was convinced that she and Tracy had discussed some things I wasn't being told. When Tracy and I got into the parking lot I was convinced of it. We got into a discussion about Jada's education – the discussion clearly highlighted our difference in philosophies and priorities in the area of education.

"Next school year Jada is going to attend Hillcrest Academy," Tracy proclaimed, as we stood in the schools parking lot.

"Why?" I asked.

"Because I believe it would be a good environment for her." Tracy boldly responded.

"That makes no sense. Jada has been struggling in the public school she attends. The curriculum at Hillcrest Academy is much tougher. I think that putting her in that environment would be setting her up for failure." I replied.

"I disagree. I believe that she would get more attention in a private school setting."

Once again, I wanted to tell Tracy to shut up. I tried to hold back but I couldn't.

"Tracy spare me! You want Jada to go to Hillcrest so that you can brag to your fake ass - wanna be diva coworkers. Everybody you work with sends their kids to those same private schools for one reason and one reason only...for bragging rights." I continued, "I don't buy that shit about needing to go to a private school to make it out of New Orleans. I got my Bachelor Degree, my sister got hers, and your sister and brother got their degrees. You know what we all have in common? We all went to public schools! The school doesn't make the person – those who work the hardest usually succeed! That's where the focus needs to be – on her work ethic. Until she develops that – it doesn't matter where she goes to school."

"I disagree," Tracy replied as she examined her manicured fingernails.

"What do you mean you disagree? Tracy, I can take a child from out of the St. Bernard projects with a 4.0 GPA, and put her up against any of those private school graduates. Once they all get to college, their level of success is not based on whether or not they went to a private or public school - their level of success in college is based on one thing and one thing only...how bad do they want it!"

Tracy just stood there and listened to my little speech. I assumed that her silence was an admission that I was right. I decided to capitalize on my perceived momentum. I figured there was no better time than the present to ask Tracy for custody.

"I've asked you before, and I'm gonna ask you again, are you gonna let Jada come and live with me for one school year? I know I can get her GPA up to at least the 2.50 level. My schedule is more flexible than yours and I can work with her more than you can," I watched intently as Tracy appeared to give my proposition some consideration.

Considering the fact that Jada's teacher had just told us the child needed help, I knew that Tracy had no choice but to consider my offer. In an effort to seal the deal I even tried to appeal to Tracy's selfish side. "Look Tracy, if it's the money you're worried about – you can stop. If you let her come and live with me I won't even ask you for child support." At the risk of sounding phony I even pretended to be concerned about her lifestyle. "You've been saying you wanted to go back to school – well if Jada's with me you won't have to worry about her while you handle your business."

Tracy looked at me and then down at the ground. For a second, it appeared that I'd finally won her over. "I don't know – I gotta think about it," she replied.

"What do you mean - "you gotta think about it?" Damn girl, can't you see our child isn't doin' well in school?" I yelled and slammed my hand on the hood of my car for affect. "I don't understand you! There are men out here that don't give a damn about their children – mutha fuckas ain't paid child support in years, and don't even know how the inside of their child's classroom look. Here I am practically begging you to give me a chance at raising "our" child, and you're lookin' at me like you're retarded."

Even if I was getting close to convincing Tracy I was right – my outburst blew it. She rolled her eyes and started looking in her purse for her car keys. I could sense I was loosing her so I went for broke.

"You've had six years to get her grades right, and this child has struggled every single year in school. You'd rather watch her struggle before you let me take a shot at getting her straight. What's wrong Tracy? Are you scared I'm gonna actually do a good job and make you look bad?"

Tracy avoided making eye contact with me as she blew a bubble with the gum she was chewing. She stared across the parking lot at a group of kids, and purposely tried to look like she was oblivious to my little diatribe.

"Tracy you're either gonna be part of the solution or part of the problem. Right about now, you're lookin' like a woman who doesn't give a damn about her child's education. All you're worried about is how you're gonna look as a mother...that's some selfish shit!" I yelled, as I pointed my finger in his face. "Actually, I think it's worse than that. I didn't want to believe this, but the way you're actin' I believe Greg was right – all you're worried about is getting' those damn child support checks."

"Whatever! Why are you so set on havin' her come live with you?" Tracy asked. "Sounds like you're lookin' for a way to get out of payin' child support. And how can Greg comment on somethin' with his "deadbeat" ass? You're stupid for listenin' to anything his "dog" ass has to say!" Tracy yelled as her nostrils flared and veins protruded from her temple.

As we both stood there with our arms folded, a school security guard drove by on a golf cart, and asked if everything was okay. Tracy said, "yes" and the security guard drove away.

I knew that Tracy had already made up her mind to send Jada to Hillcrest, but I was determined to make my position on the issue known.

"Do you know how much that school cost? The money it's gonna cost to send her to Hillcrest could be placed in a college fund. Besides, how are you gonna pay for Hillcrest? You don't even earn ten dollars an hour?"

Tracy just stood there silently. Her body language sent me into another verbal assault.

"Ya see Tracy, that's part of your problem. You got champagne taste on a Kool-Aid budget," I yelled.

"I'm gonna use the child support check to pay for Hillcrest," Tracy mumbled as she continued to look away.

"Ain't that a bitch?!" I shouted. "So what you're really sayin' is that I'm gonna pay for Hillcrest. You're gonna take the money I send you every month, and use it to pay for a school that I don't want her to go to. Then you're gonna walk around here with your damn chest stuck out tellin' everybody (including Jada) that you're the one paying for that damn school when you know that you're using my money."

At that point, I was yelling so loud that the security officer made another drive by.

"That money is for me to take care of her. If I use it to send her to the best schools than that's my business," Tracy yelled – with one hand on her hip and neck swaying from side-to-side.

"Bitch you must have fell and bumped your head. You ain't talkin' to one of your tired ass girlfriends. I know better than anybody that you've never gave a damn about that child's education – you're just worried about "keepin' up with the Jones'" and whoever else you think you can impress. If you cared about her education you'd be tryin' to do what's right."

"I do care about my child's education!"

"Yeah right. So let me ask you this - should I expect another child support increase real soon? I know how you operate. You're gonna use my hard earned money to send her to a school that I don't want her to go to, and then turn right around and hit me up for more money."

Tracy just stood there with her arms crossed. It was plain to see that she didn't care about my protest. I could feel myself drifting out of control. I snatched Tracy's car keys out of her hand to make sure I had her attention.

"Jamal give me back my keys."

"I ain't givin' you shit until you agree to let her come live with me."

"Nigga you got five seconds to give me back my keys or else I'm gonna call that security guard."

"I don't give a fuuuuuck! Call that old ass guard. I know one thing – you're gonna answer me."

Before Tracy could respond I could feel someone grab my right arm – it was Jada's teacher. She had been watching the exchange from her classroom window.

"I'm not tryin to get in ya'll business, but ya'll really should take this argument somewhere else. I just heard a parent tell someone to call the police,"

"Thank you Ms. Tillman. I'm sorry about the confusion," I replied.

When Ms. Tillman turned and walked away, I turned to Tracy and said one more thing.

"This child has not proven that she has the self discipline to study, and you are terrible at making her study. You are sending her to Hillcrest for all the wrong reasons, and the shit ain't gonna work out. Jada should attend a public school for the seventh grade, and work on improving her grades. If she shows improvement then it makes more sense to spend the money to send her to Hillcrest."

Tracy rolled her eyes, snatched her keys out of my hand, and walked off - leaving me standing in the parking lot.

"She's going to Hillcrest Academy!" she yelled, as she opened her car door and got in.

Tracy

Jamal always felt he knew more about what was best for Jada than I did. I would have probably listened to some of his suggestions if he didn't talk to me like I was some kind of an idiot.

All he talked about was his money. Sending her to Hillcrest had nothing to do with money. Everyone in New Orleans knows that the public schools are terrible. Hell, everyday on the news there's a story about some child getting jumped or robbed on the school grounds.

I ain't gonna lie, I relied on his child support money to help get me through it. But he acted like he was giving me thousands of dollars. That little $500 he was sending at that time wasn't enough to last.

I'll bet if Dawn had insisted that Jamal, Jr. attended a private school, Jamal wouldn't have protested. Nope, his hen pecked ass would have written that check without blinking an eye.

So, I didn't care about him getting mad. I'm the one who lived with Jada each day. I knew what she needed at that time. His ass was a long distance father, but if you let him tell it you'd think he was with Jada everyday. Besides, Jada was an unruly child; she needed the type of discipline that the nuns give them at Catholic schools. The public schools were overcrowded – Jada couldn't get the attention she needed.

Ultimately, I was the one who was responsible for her on a day-to-day basis, so you damn right I felt like my opinion carried more weight.

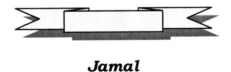

Jamal

Back in Georgia, I blossomed as an everyday dad. I appreciated the fact that I could literally see the impact I had on my son's life. I could see how being an everyday dad enabled me to help mold my son's values and decision-making process.

Throughout Jada's life I'd been there for her emotionally and financially, but it was difficult instilling my value system in her from afar. Often times, whatever I tried to teach her would be contradicted once she returned to live with her mom. By the time I saw her again, I found myself re-teaching the same rules.

I wanted to spend some time with Jada during the summer so I called and asked Tracy if she'd let Jada visit. Jada had never stayed with me for more than two consecutive weeks. Not because I didn't want more time, but because two weeks was usually all Tracy would allow.

Tracy said she missed Jada when she wasn't around, but I say the only thing she was scared of missing was that $500 child support check.

Dawn and I spent the entire two weeks preaching to Jada the importance of making up her bed and cleaning up her room every morning. At Tracy's house, Jada didn't have to clean up her room and make up her bed because Tracy took care of it.

I was content to chalk the issue up as a difference of styles – that is until Tracy asked me about it one day. Apparently, Jada mentioned that Dawn had scolded her for not cleaning up her room – Tracy wasn't having it.

"Why is your wife yellin' at my child?"

"What are you talkin' about?"

"Jada told me that Dawn yelled at her for not cleaning up her room."

"I don't know if she yelled at her, but I'm sure she made her go and do it. I make her clean up her room too."

"Well she's not used to having to do that everyday."

"Oh well, as long as she's out here she's gonna clean up her room. If you don't want her to do it than I suggest you hop on the first thing smokin' and come and clean it up for her. Bottom line, that damn room is gonna be cleaned." I barked, as I deliberately looked at Jada. My glare told her that I didn't appreciate her complaining to her mom about my rules.

"All I know is this, you'd better tell your little wife she'd better not yell at my child." Tracy responded, and then abruptly hung up the phone.

Dawn and I took Jada and Little Jamal to Six Flags. Our goal was to defuse the tension and allow Jada to have some fun. However, in the back of my mind I knew that the fight with Tracy wasn't over.

When we returned from Six Flags there was a message from Tracy on the answering machine asking me to call her.

"Yeah, wuz up?"

"Jamal I would like for Jada to come home."

"Why so soon, school doesn't start for another couple of weeks."

Tracy paused for a moment. She cleared her throat and tapped her hands on the end table next to her chair. She knew that no matter how hard she tried I was going to put up a fuss...I always did.

"I got her enrolled in Hillcrest Academy, and they start school two weeks earlier than public schools."

"So you went and did it anyway despite my feelings about the issue?"

"Jamal I heard everything you said, but this is where I want her to go."

"Oh yeah, and your decision is final because she's more your daughter than mine right?"

"Jamal I didn't call to argue with you. Could you please just bring my child home next weekend?"

"Your child! The last time I checked - your child had my last name. I'll tell you what, give me a few days to think about bringing her home."

Dawn walked over to me and tried to be the voice
of reason.

"Baby I know she gets on your nerves – trust me, I
can't stand her tired ass. But, you know she has the
upper hand. If you try to keep Jada out here Tracy is
just gonna become an even bigger bitch."

"I know that. I'm not gonna give her a reason to
call them white folks on me. I wanna make her ass
sweat for a few."

I looked at Dawn and winked. She smiled in
agreement.

"Yeah – make her ass sweat," she replied and gave
me a high-five.

Since Tracy was insisting that I bring Jada back
so soon, I knew that could only mean one thing...a
child support increase was right around the corner.
Not once had Tracy ever given me any forewarning
that she'd requested an increase. Even when we were
being cordial she'd have me served with an increase. I
hated Tracy's covert approach to requesting more
money. I thought her approach was cowardly, and it
only fueled my dislike for her.

Fortunately, I always had enough cushion in my
household budget to absorb the increases, but after
the third increase Dawn begin to get annoyed. Dawn
had always supported my relationship with Jada, but
the "baby mama" drama that Tracy brought to the
table was starting to become unbearable.

I ignored Tracy's phone calls for an entire week.
She left all kinds of threatening messages on my
answering machine. Dawn and I would listen to them
and laugh. Finally, I answered the phone when she
called one evening.

"Jamal I know you've been getting' my messages.
You'd better bring my child back here or else I'm
gonna call the police and tell them you kidnapped her.
If you think I'm playin' – try me!"

I knew she was capable of calling the cops, but I wasn't gonna let Tracy know her threat worked. I waited a few more days, and then I brought Jada home on a Saturday.

During the drive back to New Orleans I decided to ask Jada what her feelings were about the school she attended.

"Jada, I know your mama wants you to go to Hillcrest Academy – what do you want?"

"I don't wanna go."

"Why?"

"Cause I don't wanna wear the uniform."

"You ever told your mama that?"

"Yeah, but she always tells me – too bad!"

We arrived in New Orleans at 5:00 p.m. I helped Jada get her clothes out of my car, and brought them to her bedroom. When we entered Jada's room I saw several Hillcrest Academy uniforms sprawled across the bed. Tracy stayed as far away from me as possible.

As I walked towards the front door I noticed some pictures laying on the coffee table. Initially, I ignored the photos, but at second glance I recognized a guy I knew named Mannie on one of the photos.

Mannie was a high school buddy of mine who was serving a seven-year sentence in the federal penitentiary for drug trafficking. At one time, Mannie and I were pretty close, but as with many childhood friendships, we grew apart as we got older.

After I joined the Marines I'd heard rumors that Tracy started dating Mannie. Tracy always denied it. These photos taken of the two of them were proof that she'd been lying to me about their relationship.

I was about to walk out when I noticed a photo of Tracy, Mannie, and Jada. Mannie (wearing his orange jailhouse jumpsuit) was holding Jada in his arms while Tracy stood next to him smiling from ear to ear.

"What the fuck is Jada doing in a picture with you and Mannie?" I asked, as I held up the photo.

"Those pictures are about three years old," Tracy nervously replied.

"I wouldn't give a damn if the pictures were 30 years old. Why in the hell would you take her to a federal prison to see Mannie?" I asked and then threw the photo to the floor.

"He asked to see her, and since I was going up there I decided to bring her. What's the big deal?" Tracy responded.

"What's the big deal?! The big deal is that you took my daughter to see a man that's in jail. First of all, I'm her daddy and you had no right takin' my child to a damn prison without talking to me first. Secondly, there is only one man on this planet she should be visiting at a prison, and that's me. Since I ain't in jail, that child should have never been exposed to a prison you jackass!"

Tracy was startled by my tone and body language. She grabbed the handle of a broom that was leaning on the wall next to her. She wasn't sure what she was going to do with it, but she knew I was in rare form and she needed to be prepared for anything. She wanted me to get as far away as possible.

"Whatever! Jamal get out of my house before I call the police."

Once again, I felt that Tracy had disrespected my role as Jada's father and I was fed up. I lunged towards her, but a sofa that was positioned in the center of the room blocked my path. Tracy ran into the kitchen and grabbed a large knife.

As I made my way around the sofa Jada came into the room. I could see in her eyes that the child was terrified. I looked at Jada and then looked at Tracy.

"Go back into your room Jada!" I yelled.

Jada shook her head and said, "Daddy, don't hurt my mama."

The tears in Jada's eyes were all I needed to see to regain my composure. I went to the coffee table and grabbed all of the photos with Jada on them with Mannie. I started to tear up every photo, but before I tore up the last one I turned to Jada.

"Do you know who this is?"

"Yeah!" Jada replied, as tears streamed down her face.

"What do you know about this man?" I asked like a police detective interrogating a witness.

Jada started crying profusely as she looked over at Tracy who was still standing in the kitchen holding the large knife.

"That's...that's...that's Uncle Mannie!" she answered.

I turned to Tracy and said, "You got her trained well."

I went back to my car, and got the rest of Jada's things. Rather than re-enter the apartment, I left her clothes at the entrance to the front door. I wanted to say good-bye to Jada, but I tried to avoid entering Tracy's apartment again – so I left.

After leaving Tracy's house I headed straight for the interstate in route to Georgia. I was so angry that I ran through a red light and damn near hit a pedestrian crossing the street. During the trip several thoughts ran through my mind:

Why would she bring Jada to see Mannie in prison? Before he went to jail, Mannie was making a lot of money hustling. Was he giving Tracy money for Jada? Is he Jada's real dad?

I made the seven-hour drive from New Orleans to Atlanta in six hours. When I got back to my house there was a letter sitting on the kitchen table addressed to me. The letter was from the Child Support Enforcement office. Right before I opened up the letter I got a pain in my stomach. I knew it was another increase; I just wasn't sure how much it would be. I continued to open the letter, and sure enough, my payments had been increased by $100 a month.

It was midway through Jada's seventh grade year, and I had only heard from her twice. Both times I had initiated contact by calling Tracy's house. I could sense that Jada was becoming more and more distant. The times when I did talk to her the conversation was strained, and Jada seemed in a hurry to get off of the phone. I was hurt by Jada's attitude change, but tried not to let it show.

Every time I hung up the phone I felt rejected and dejected because either Jada didn't want to talk or my phone call went unanswered.

Dawn was always there to provide support. She would rub my shoulders and tell me not to worry about it, but I couldn't help but feel that Tracy had succeeded at turning the child against me. Finally, I decided to stop calling, and wait for Jada to call me.

Two months later I received an honorable discharge from the military. My mother had been diagnosed as having cancer a few months earlier, and I wanted to be closer to her so I relocated back to New Orleans. I also felt that returning to New Orleans would help me re-establish a relationship with my daughter.

I spent the first few weeks in New Orleans looking for a job and trying to adjust to my newfound freedom as a civilian. I took a job as an investigator for a small insurance company. After six months of working there and dealing with the nepotism and racism, I decided to pursue my own entrepreneurial dreams.

I took $10,000 of the $20,000 I had saved up, and invested in a fledgling barbershop. I had no intentions of becoming a barber, but I knew that there was a profit to be made in the city of New Orleans if I worked at it.

I converted the barbershop into a coed barbershop and beauty salon. I bribed some of the finest barbers and hair stylist I could find into coming to work for me, and we never looked back.

Within one year the place was the classiest spot in the city. We did everything from offer car washes to serve meals while our customers got their hair and faces done. On Friday evening the place was like a nightclub. By the end of the first year in business I was making plans to open my second location – in Atlanta.

Unfortunately, I still hadn't heard from Jada, and although I knew making the first attempt to contact the child was the mature thing to do, I couldn't help but be bitter at the fact that I had to beg this child for some attention. Even so, I called Tracy's house and left my phone number and address on her answering machine.

Two weeks after leaving my phone number and address I still hadn't received any phone calls from Jada. Rather than continuing to sit by the phone and wait for Jada to acknowledge me, I focused all of my energy and time on my family, my mother, and my new businesses. One Friday evening while reviewing a business proposal I was preparing for a prospective client the phone rang...it was Jada.

"Hello Daddy."

I was torn – a part of me was happy to hear from her, but the other part wanted to give her a tongue-lashing.

"So you finally decided to call? How are you doing?"

"I was just calling to let you know that I passed to the eighth grade."

"That's good, but is that all you called to tell me? Why haven't you called before tonight? Did you get the messages I left for you?" "What messages? I never got any..."

Before Jada could finish her sentence, Tracy snatched the phone from her and started talking.

"Jamal did she tell you that she's been kicked out of Hillcrest Academy?"

"What do you mean kicked out? The school year is over."

"Yeah she made it through the year, but her grade point average was so low that the people sent me a letter saying that she couldn't return next year."

I knew that I should have been expressing some type of remorse or sorrow, but I couldn't let this moment pass without rubbing it in Tracy's face.

"Oh well, I told you she wasn't ready for that school's curriculum, but you had to send her there to impress your friends. So what are you gonna do about next year? Where are you..."

Before I could finish my sentence Tracy had given the phone back to Jada. I was mad that Tracy didn't hear me out, but I wasn't surprised. Tracy repeatedly made bad decisions regarding Jada, but never wanted to be held accountable. Her reluctance to listen to me gloat was vindication enough. I tried to focus on consoling Jada. I could hear sniffling as if she'd been crying,

"Jada what's wrong?"

"Daddy I tried hard this year." Jada replied as she tried to hold back her tears.

"I know that you did. The fact that you passed is what's most important. Since I live here now, next school year will be better because I'm gonna be able to help you with your homework more okay. Stop crying, and I'm gonna come and get you tomorrow so that we can go to dinner and spend some time together."

"Okay. Daddy I'm sorry I didn't call you."

"Don't worry about it baby girl - I'll see you tomorrow at 10:00 a.m."

After spending four years in New Orleans, Dawn and I realized that we had outgrown the city. Yeah we enjoyed many of the events such as: Mardi Gras, Jazz Festival, Essence Festival, and the food - but the city's economy and job market were depressing. My salons were doing okay, but we hated living in the city. After much deliberation we decided to relocate to Texas to take advantage of the booming real estate market.

I sold my salons and relocated to Dallas. I hooked up with a guy I knew and started refurbishing old houses. It wasn't long before I opened my own Real Estate and Property Management Company. My annual take home salary was near the six-figure mark, and things were really beginning to look up. I built a 4,500 square foot home in the suburbs of Dallas, along with all of the spoils of success (i.e., Mercedes Benz, Rolex watch, etc.).

Unfortunately, along with the success came the usual "baby mama" drama. As soon as Tracy got wind of my prosperity, she damn near sprained an ankle running to the child support office to ask for an increase. At this point, I didn't even care. I knew that Tracy's extortion days were running out. Jada was seventeen years old, and Tracy's days of living high off of my money were coming to an end.

In Texas I spent most of my time focusing on new business ventures. I was determined to break into the day spa and child daycare industry. With the real estate connections I had made during the past few years, I knew I could get the types of leases for my businesses that would enable me to break-even quickly.

I opened my first day spa in a building I'd purchased at an auction. The previous owner had attempted to open up a spa, but ran out of financial support and was forced to file for bankruptcy less than six months after he opened. When the bank kicked him out, he left most of the furniture in the building. I purchased the building and all of its contents and hit the ground running. Within one year I had positioned my day spa as the premier location for professional African-Americans in the metropolitan Dallas area.

Back on the home front things weren't operating as smoothly. Jada and Tracy were having a difficult time living under the same roof. It seemed as though once a week I had been getting phone calls from Tracy complaining about Jada. Tracy was accusing Jada of sneaking boys into the house and failing in school. Tracy even sent me copies of letters from Jada's school (another private school that my child support check was paying for), stating that Jada was close to failing the 11th grade.

The proverbial "shit hit the fan" when Jada called me crying hysterically one Monday night. Jada said that Tracy was putting her out of the house, and sending her to Dallas to live with me. To describe my reaction as "stunned" would be an understatement.

I had more than enough room in my home, but I wasn't expecting this. Having gone through this time and time again with Tracy and Jada over the years, I proceeded with caution.

"What do you mean she's putting you out?" I asked Jada in a very cavalier voice.

"She told me to pack my bags because I was coming to live with you." Jada replied hysterically.

"Where is your mom?"

"She's on the phone with the airlines buying a ticket."

"What happened?"

"I don't know. She just started tripping! At first she was accusing me of leaving school early, and when I told her that wasn't true she slapped me."

I rolled my eyes and asked, "And what did you do?"

Much to my surprise Jada replied, "I hit her back, and then we started fighting. When we stopped she told me I had to leave."

I had reached a point where nothing surprised me when it came to those two.

"So when is she saying you have to leave so I can make arrangements to come and get you?"

"She said I had to leave tonight. My aunt is here, and she's taking me to her house tonight. I'll be leaving for the airport tomorrow morning. Will you be able to pick me up from the airport?" Jada asked.

Suddenly I begin to take this little episode more seriously. I stuttered for a moment as I searched for words.

"Of course you can come and live with us. Just call me when your flight leaves New Orleans, and I'll leave to go to the airport here in Dallas."

I still wasn't sure if Jada was really being kicked out. I knew that Tracy was extremely temperamental, and that she had a bad habit of speaking first, and then feeling sorry about what she said after she'd calm down. I figured that by the next morning Tracy would have come to her senses and realized that kicking the child out of the house with two months remaining in the school year was not only irresponsible...it was down right stupid.

At approximately 7:00 a.m. that next morning, I was awakened by a phone call from Jada. She was at the New Orleans airport and was minutes away from boarding a plane to Dallas. I said okay, but I still wouldn't believe it until I saw Jada with my own two eyes.

I got Jada's flight information and went to the airport in Dallas. When Jada walked out of the terminal I was surprised, angry, and concerned.

I was surprised to see that my 17-year-old daughter had the body and face of a 21-year-old college senior. I was angry because I thought that kicking the child out during the school year was by far the most irresponsible thing Tracy had ever done. My concern was the byproduct of seeing that Jada had only one bag in her possession.

I gave her a hug and put her bag into my SUV.

"Are you okay? Where are the rest of your bags?" I asked.

"I'm okay. That's the only bag I have. She told me that if what I was taking couldn't fit in that bag than I was just out of luck. She refused to let me bring anything else," Jada replied.

I was wise enough to know that there had to be more to this story than what I was being told so I used the ride home to try to get to the truth. As we pulled away from the curb we both looked at each other as if we were seeing a ghost. Neither of us could believe that it had come to this.

"I don't know what happened between you and your mom, but whatever you did it must have been pretty bad."

"Daddy I didn't do anything. Remember when I talked to you last week, and I told you that I wanted to come live with you? Well, apparently she was recording our phone conversation. She repeated everything we talked about, and then she told me that if I wanted to live with you I should start packing my stuff."

"So what did you say?"

"I said yes, I want to go live with my daddy. When I said that she just clicked! She started accusing me of skipping out on school and then she walked towards me and slapped me in my face."

I took pride in my ability to handle stressful situations and make quick decisions, but I must admit - I was somewhat overwhelmed by this sudden change of events. I had absolutely no faith in anything Tracy said, but I also knew of Jada's propensity to lie. Rather than wasting time trying to figure out where the truth stopped and the lying begin, I decided to concentrate on the things I thought were more important – things like: getting Jada enrolled in school, buying her some more clothes, and getting her braces removed just for starters.

Jada and I stopped at a local diner to eat breakfast. I started smiling as I watched her maul the pancake she'd ordered. Deep in my heart I knew that I could run circles around Tracy in the parenting department, and now I was going to get the opportunity to show it. I felt that this might have been a blessing in disguise.

My immediate goal was to get Jada enrolled in school. I spent the entire next day planning and making phone calls. I assumed I had everything under control, but I had no idea of the stress that awaited me - two days later I hit my first roadblock.

I attempted to enroll Jada in the high school located less than two miles from my home. This public high school was less than four years old, and it was fabulous. The building was state of the art. It had a football stadium that held up to 10,000 people, a baseball stadium, Olympic size track, six tennis courts, and an indoor football practice field with artificial turf.

The school offered over 30 different electives for the students (ranging from horticulture to cosmetology to archeology). This public high school was better than any public or private high school in New Orleans. As a matter of fact, it was fancier than most of the colleges in the city of New Orleans.

I met with the principal of the school, and explained the conditions surrounding Jada being sent here. The principal sympathized with my predicament, and agreed to let Jada enroll and take junior level classes. However, the woman made it clear to me that Jada would not be allowed to start the next school year as a senior unless I could produce transcripts from Jada's previous school. If I didn't produce those transcripts Jada would be classified as a freshman or maybe a sophomore at best -depending on how many credits they could transfer.

I agreed to contact Jada's former school, and have her transcripts sent immediately. It seemed like a relatively easy task, and I figured that even if Jada was forced to repeat some classes it couldn't hurt her.

Tracy still hadn't learned her lesson from the Hillcrest Academy fiasco because she enrolled Jada in another "private" all-girls school for her eleventh grade year - Tompkins Academy. When I contacted Tompkins, I was directed to the finance department. I found this odd because I didn't understand how retrieving transcripts had anything to do with finances.

The Director of the Financial Aid Department (Ms. Lovelace) answered and I introduced himself, "Hi my name is Jamal Simms, and my daughter Jada Simms is a former student there. I was wondering what I would need to do to have her transcripts sent here to Texas."

Ms. Lovelace was kind but very direct.

"Before we can send anything your daughter's account will have to be settled."

"What do you mean?" I asked.

"There is a $1,200 dollar balance on your daughter's account. The tuition hasn't been paid in three months. I spoke to your ex-wife Tracy Newhouse last week, and she said she would catch up on the bill." Ms. Lovelace replied.

I quickly corrected the lady, "First of all she's not my ex-wife - we just have a child together. Secondly, I wasn't aware that there was a balance on her account. I'm going to call Tracy and find out what's going on. Thank you for your time Ms. Lovelace, I'll call you back later on today."

I hung up the phone and as you might guess – I was pissed off. I sent Tracy $800 a month and she told me that she was using $400 each month to pay Jada's tuition. I immediately begin to wonder:

What is she doing with my money? Jada told me that Tracy only gives her $50 each month; so what is she doing with the rest of my money?

I knew that there was only one way to find out, so I called Tracy at work. Tracy admitted that the account was in arrears, but denied only giving Jada $50 a month. Tracy avoided explaining why the account was delinquent, so I asked her to pay the balance on the account so that the school would release Jada's transcripts. Tracy said that she would pay the balance by May 15th. I was okay with this agreement because I knew that I'd worked out the deal with Jada's new school to let her attend 11th grade classes for the final four weeks of the school year. However, I knew that Jada would be up "shit creek" if Tracy didn't pay that balance before August 15th.

The summer came and went in a flash. Before I knew it August had arrived, and I needed to get Jada ready for her senior year. I spoke to Ms. Lovelace at Jada's former school. It seems that Tracy still hadn't paid the balance; therefore, the school was still refusing to send Jada's transcripts.

Tracy had not attempted to contact Jada during the entire summer. I was starting to get desperate so I decided to call Tracy's job one morning to ask her once again when she intended to pay the balance on the account.

"Hello, may I speak to Tracy," I asked.

"Tracy no longer works here – she hasn't worked here in months," replied the lady that answered the phone.

I immediately called Tracy's home phone number, but the operator said the phone had been disconnected. I could feel another migraine headache coming on. Tracy had changed jobs and phone numbers since we last spoke, and didn't bother to let me know. What made it worse was the fact that she still hadn't paid the balance on Jada's account. I was between a rock and a hard place. The new school year was less than two weeks away, and I still did not have Jada's transcripts.

I knew that I could afford to pay the $1,200 balance, but I didn't feel I should have to. Tracy was the one who decided to send the child to that private school, and Tracy was the one who signed the promissory note. As far as I was concerned, that was Tracy's bill – not mine.

Although the school would have gladly accepted a check from anyone, I couldn't stomach the idea of paying off Tracy's account. To make matters worse, I had Dawn giving me the "you'd better not pay that heifer's bill" look.

I was at a crossroads. Jada had not attended a public school since her ninth grade year; therefore, those were the only transcripts the new school could retrieve. Her tenth and eleventh grade years were spent at Tompkins Academy, and those records were unattainable as long as there was an outstanding balance. To say I was in a predicament was an understatement. If I didn't pay the tuition bill Jada would be demoted from a senior down to a freshman. If I did pay the bill then Tracy would be freed of her financial obligation. She would have killed two birds with one stone – avoided paying her own bill and dodged having to explain the whereabouts of the missing $1,200 dollars in child support money.

I carefully weighed my options. At one point I thought about paying two of my wild ass female cousins to go over to Tracy's house and whip her ass until she gave up her ATM card and pin number. That thought vanished when I thought about the cousins I had in mind – they were borderline crazies. If Tracy attempted to fight back they might just kill her. Although, I hated the ground Tracy walked on, she wasn't worth a murder in the first-degree conviction. In the end, I decided to do what I thought was best for Jada...I paid the $1,200 balance.

My next task was to have Jada's braces removed. I had Jada's braces installed more than four years earlier. During that time I was paying $100 a month (non-refundable) for monthly upkeep, but stopped making the payments because Tracy kept forgetting to bring Jada to the scheduled appointments.

During the course of one year, Jada missed eight Orthodontist appointments. As I drove Jada to meet the new Orthodontist I anticipated him querying me about the condition of Jada's teeth. The thought of being chastised by this man caused me to think back to my comments to Tracy regarding the braces:

Tracy I spoke to the receptionist at the dentist office today, and she informed me that Jada has missed 8 of her last 12 dentist appointments. She told me that the money I sent to cover those appointments Jada missed is non-refundable. Since you don't seem to give a fuck about me wasting my money, you can pay for the damn braces. I've already instructed them to send any future bills to you.

In typical fashion, Tracy arrogantly told me she'd take care of Jada's braces - two weeks later I received a letter from the Child Support Enforcement office. The letter politely informed me that my child support payments had been increased by $100 a month...the same amount as the dentist fee.

Obviously the increase in child support Tracy received was not used on Jada's teeth because the braces still hadn't been removed. Jada's teeth were turning gray. It pained me to see the embarrassment in her face. I could not let my child start a new school as a senior with her teeth looking like this.

Teenagers can be cruel. I remembered how my friends and I would tease each other constantly. To see guys on the verge of crying from the ribbing was commonplace. Jada was entering her senior year and I wanted her to do well and be happy I didn't want her to be a social outcast.

Since Jada's condition was considered "pre-existing" my insurance wouldn't cover it. I was told that it would cost $1,500 to have the braces removed. I cringed at the thought of shelling out another large sum of money. That would be $2,700 in one week, but out of love for Jada, I begrudgingly paid the fee.

Jada was excited about finally having her braces removed. The look of joy on her face made me happy. When I went to get Jada from the orthodontist office, the receptionist told me that Dr. Watkins needed to meet with me.

I wasn't sure what he wanted to discuss, but I knew it couldn't have been anything good. Dr. Watkins met me in the hallway outside of my office.

"Mr. Simms I removed Jada's braces, but it appears that they have been on far too long. Jada did not do a good job of cleaning her teeth, and as a result, it appears that she may have a couple of cavities. I would highly recommend that you have her see a dentist as soon as possible."

I was not happy. I anticipated there would be some damage to her teeth, but judging from Dr.

Watkins' demeanor, the damage was going to be worse than I thought. I made an appointment with my family dentist so that Jada could have the cavities taken care of. Once my dentist looked at Jada's teeth, I found myself sitting in another conference.

"Jamal, I have to say this...I've been practicing my trade for 13 years now, and I'll be honest with you, this is the worse case of neglect I've ever seen. That child has 8 cavities. She is going to need a root canal, two fillings, and at least five crowns for her front teeth. I realize that you inherited this problem, but I must tell you, we really need to start working on this as soon as possible."

I was shocked and embarrassed; I had no idea Jada's dental problems were that extensive. To make matters worse, my dentist told me that Jada need more than $3,000 worth of cosmetic dental work. My dental plan only covered $1,500 worth of work a year per family member; therefore, I had to pay the balance.

I wrote the dentist a check for $1,500 and asked him to fit Jada in as soon as possible to get the work started. He instructed his assistant to find a way to fit Jada in. It normally took weeks to get an appointment at this man's office - the urgency he displayed let me know how severe Jada's situation was.

Needless to say, I was not a happy camper. I was starting to wonder if Tracy had sent Jada to me so that she could avoid having to pay for all of these expenses.

I went home and pulled out my checkbook. When I tallied up the receipts from the shopping spree, school transcripts, and dentist - I discovered that I'd already spent $4,200 on Jada in three months.

Although the figure bothered me – I was more disturbed at Jada's seemingly cavalier attitude towards the money I'd spent on her behalf. I couldn't remember her showing any overt signs of gratitude – no hugs or kisses.

I could feel my anger mounting when suddenly there was a knock at my office door – it was Jada. She entered the room and stood against the wall. She seemed afraid to make eye contact with me as she mumbled the words – *thank you.*

Dawn

I had so much on my mind during that time that I hadn't taken the time to return phone calls or take care of little things around the house. I needed to call my best friend Wanda back. Wanda's a corporate lawyer with no children, no husband, and will tell you in a heartbeat – she's happily single.

Wanda called me weeks earlier, but I wasn't able to talk to her. I needed to call "my girl" to make sure everything was okay.

"What's up Wanda?"

"Dawn is that you?"

"Yeah it's me."

"Baaaaby, I thought your ass died or somethin' – I called you a month ago."

"I know – girl I've been dealin' with a whole lotta shit out here. What's up with you?"

"I'm trying to get ready for my date."

"Still gettin' your date on?"

"You know it! Baaaaby, I'm happy being single. Married people I know seem to be miserable – always complaining about their man. Shit, I can do bad by myself - I don't need any help. Never mind that, what's up with you? The last time we talked you started to tell me that Jada had moved in with ya'll, but you never finished tellin' me what happened."

"Girl I don't even know where to start. That child got more drama with her than you'd believe."

I paused for a moment before I continued. Wanda and I had been friends since high school. I used to hang with her back when Jamal and I first started to date. She used to always try to discourage me from dating him because he had a child while we were still in high school. She never stopped being my friend, but she made her thoughts about my marrying Jamal very clear – she thought it was a big mistake.

Wanda was a kind person, but she had a steadfast rule that she would not date a man with children – not even one child. In her opinion, the "baby mama drama" wasn't worth the headaches. Naturally, I was reluctant to tell her about everything that had been going on in my household, but I needed to talk to someone I could trust.

"Wanda I feel like our lives have been turned upside down."

"What has that crazy bitch Tracy done now?"

"Wanda she kicked that child out of her house."

"Well I figured that – why else would Jada come to live with ya'll?"

"No, you're not feelin' me – she kicked that child out with no clothes – just the clothes on her back."

"You're lying?"

"Girl, when Jamal picked Jada up at the airport the child had one of those little suitcases that you see flight attendants walkin' around with – that's it."

"That's a damn shame! I know Jamal cut up."

"You know how Jamal is about that child. He was pissed off."

"I know girl, I'll bet he lost it."

"He was furious. He went and spent hundreds of dollars the next day on clothes for Jada. The girl had nothing when she got here, but she got a bunch of shit now."

Before I told her more I paused for a second to take a sip of my lemonade to sooth my parched mouth.

"Wanda – the shit gets deeper."

"Deeper? Well let me turn off this television so I can hear it all."

"Girl let me tell you…"

"Wait a second, I told you I gotta get right so I can hear everything. I gotta use the bathroom first – do you wanna hold on for a second or call me back?"

"Girl hurry up and go pee – Jamal's gonna be home in a few minutes and I gotta tell you this!"

"Alright, alright, give a sista a second."

A few moments later Wanda returned to the phone.

"Dee this had better be a good story – you got me rushin' my pee – you know that shit hurts."

"Be quiet and listen. Jamal ended up paying Tompkins Academy $1,200 to release Jada's transcripts."

"Why did he do that?"

"Because Tracy owed the school money and they refused to release the transcripts until the debt was paid. It was the only way we could get the child enrolled in school as a senior. If he didn't pay it the school was going to put her in the 9th grade."

"Why?"

"Because that's the last time she attended a public school. We could get her transcripts from a public school, but those private schools want their money first."

"So let me get this straight – Jamal pays Tracy child support every month. I assume she uses some of the child support check to pay for that school. But, she didn't use the money for the school; therefore, the tuition was overdue. So Jamal ends up paying the child support and Jada's tuition bill...that's foul!"

"You think that's foul – listen to this. When was the last time you saw Jada?"

"I don't know I guess it's been about three years."

"Do you remember you saw us in the mall that day?"

"Yeah, I think that may have been the last time I saw her."

"Well, you might remember that she had braces on her teeth."

"I do remember that. I remember teasing her a little."

"Well guess what was still on her teeth when she came here.'

"Dawn I know that child wasn't wearing those braces?"

"Yes she was. Tracy had stopped taking the child to the Orthodontist."

"Dawn that means she had those things in her mouth for nearly four years. Wait a minute, didn't you tell me Jamal paid for the braces."

"I told you Jamal paid to have them put in her mouth. He and Tracy got into a big argument a few years ago because she wasn't taking Jada to the Orthodontist regularly. Jamal was paying the Orthodontist for visits that Jada wasn't making. He got mad and stopped paying. Tracy got mad at him because he "checked" her ass about the situation – so she went down to the child support office the next week and requested an increase."

"Let me guess, they gave her an increase which means Jamal still ended up paying for the braces?"

"You know it!"

"Ya see - that's why I don't mess with any man that has a child. My nerves are bad – I'd end up killin' him and his "baby mama.""

"I feel you girl! Anyway, the shit has gotten crazier. Jada comes out here and still has the braces on her teeth. We weren't sure how much damage had been done, but we figured it was gonna be extensive."

"Girl you know I had braces in my mouth when we were teenagers. You can't leave those things in that long."

"Wanda, we took that girl to the Orthodontist and had those braces removed and I swear I almost cried. You know how beautiful Jada is – that child's mouth was ruined."

"Oh no!"

"Yes girlfriend! That child had so many rotten teeth in her mouth she was too embarrassed to smile.'

"What did ya'll do?"

"Jamal became obsessed with getting Jada's teeth fixed. The problem is, at that time Jamal had a lot of money tied up in all of these business ventures; so he was forced to cash in my baby's college fund so that he could come up with the money to pay the dentist."

"Well how much did it cost?"

"It cost $1,500 in cash just to get the Orthodontist to look at her mouth and eventually remove the braces."

"Ya'll don't have dental insurance?"

"Yes we have dental insurance, but that was a pre-existing condition – our insurance wouldn't cover it. We were able to put all of the cosmetic work that they had to do on our insurance plan, but that still cost us another $1,500 in co-pay fees."

"Girl, you got a good man because most brotha's would have let her ass walk around looking like "yuck mouth." I ain't gonna lie – that's a lot of money to be shelling out unexpectedly. I might have made her ass go toothless."

"Wanda don't say that."

"I'm serious! Her mama is a hustler. She has been milking Jamal for money all these years and apparently spending the money on everything but what the hell she is supposed to spend it on. Dawn, I know you're supportive of Jamal, but you can't tell me you weren't pissed when he cashed in your baby's college fund to pay for that dental work?"

"Hell yeah I was pissed! But what am I supposed to do?"

"I'll tell you what you should do, you should come down here and we can roll up on that heifer's job. I never liked her ass anyway."

"I wouldn't mind doin' that, but I don't know where she works. She changed jobs and now we have absolutely no way of getting in touch with her. But you know what pisses me off even more?"

"What's that?"

"Jada acts like she can care less about the sacrifices Jamal is making."

"'She hasn't thanked him? You need to go snatch her little ass."

"Trust me – a part of me wants to. I approached Jada as she sat watching television in her bedroom, and I asked her if she realized the hoops her daddy had to jump through to get her into school and get her teeth fixed?"

"What did she say?"

"Girl, she just sat there with this blank look on her face. I wanted to slap the shit outta her!"

"You should have. She sounds like she might have some of her mama's traits."

"Girl, eventually she looked up at me and said she understood, but I can tell that she hadn't given it any thought prior to me confronting her."

"What did you do?"

"I told her that before the end of the day, she'd better make an effort to thank her daddy for all that he has done."

"It's a damn shame that you had to have a conversation like that with a 17 year old child. You'd think she'd have enough common sense to not bite the hand that's feeding, clothing, and providing for her."

"Yeah you would think that, but you know good sense ain't common."

"You're right about that."

"Girl, I can tell already that this ain't gonna work out."

"Oh, you had better believe that Tracy knew what the hell she was doing. Yeah she got ya'll good."

"What do you mean?"

"Girl can't you see? Tracy kicked that child out at the perfect time. Jada was probably going through typical teenage girl stuff – which we know can drive a mother crazy. Combine that with having to pay for the private school and braces and all the other expensive shit that's comes with a teenage girl and there you have it. Correct me if I'm wrong, but isn't Tracy engaged now?"

"Yeah, she's getting married soon."

"Girl, you don't even have to tell me anything else – I see right through that tramp's plan. She needed to unload that headache. Baaaaby, Jada will be turnin' 18 pretty soon. That means those damn child support checks are about to stop coming. Jada is no longer an asset – now she's a liability. What do you do with a liability? You get rid of it. Trust me, Tracy knew that Jamal would be right there to take over. I'm telling you Dee, Tracy is..."

Wanda's comments were cut short by the apparent arrival of her date.

"...Dee – we're gonna have to finish this conversation later. But let me say this before I go. I know I gave you a hard time about marrying Jamal, but I gotta tell you – you got a good man. Most brothas wouldn't do a fraction of the things he's done for that child. Don't let Jada's trifling ass mama mess up your happy home. I gotta go sweetie, but we'll continue this convo soon."

"Girl thanks for listenin' to me vent – you go and have fun."

Before I could hang up the phone I heard the front door open – Jamal had made it home. It was time to put on the supportive wife face. Time to massage his shoulders and reassure him that everything was going to work out. Time to tell him that his mother is watching from above and would be proud of the way he's handled everything.

I'd never told Jamal how I really felt about everything that had transpired. We never really talked about the situation – welcoming Jada into our home just seemed like the logical and moral thing to do. But, I must admit that I wasn't happy with the changes. I wasn't happy with the tension that existed. I wasn't happy with the lack of affection between Jamal and I. We used to laugh a lot, go out on dates, rent movies, make love often – but once Jada arrived all that changed. I never realized how much the transition bothered me until I spoke to Wanda. It wasn't until I spoke to Wanda that I realized I was one of those unhappily married people she talked about.

Chapter 7 - The Truth Hurts

Jamal

The school year was well underway, and as much as I hated to admit it, with each passing day my daughter would prove her mother's allegations to be true. Within the first two months of school, I caught Jada lying on at least four different occasions. Each time, the lie being told was more devious than the previous. The lies ranged from sneaking on the phone late at night to cutting classes to sneaking boys in my house.

At first I was prepared to chalk this incident up as typical teenage poor judgment, but my wife Dawn wasn't so forgiving. With each stunt Dawn became more and more distrustful of Jada, and it started becoming increasingly apparent to me that my wife wanted my daughter gone.

One day I received a call from Jada's guidance counselor.

"Mr. Simms I just wanted to extend my condolences."

"Condolences - I'm not sure I understand what you are talking about." I responded.

"One of Jada's classmates came to me crying. The child was upset because Jada said she was going to kill herself now that her mother had died."

"Ms. Lowery can I come meet with you in person?"

"Sure Mr. Simms, I'll be in my office after 3 p.m. – we can talk about Jada's frame of mind. We want to help her in anyway we can."

I hung up the phone in a state of shock. Suicide – Tracy was dead – what in the hell was this lady talking about? I didn't know what was going on, but I was going to find out.

"Hello Mr. Simms – I'm glad you could come by."

"I'm glad you agreed to meet with me."

"Of course, I just want to help Jada in anyway I can. She obviously isn't handling the death well."

"Ms. Lowery I'm embarrassed to say this, but Jada's mother isn't dead. Jada and her mother haven't spoken to each other in five months. Jada's mother put her out – that's why she's living with me now."

Ms. Lowery stared at me with a horrified look on her face. It was apparent that Jada's lie ranked amongst the worst she'd ever heard.

"Mr. Simms – I don't know what to say. I assumed that this alleged death had a lot to do with Jada's poor grades."

"What poor grades?" I asked. Suddenly, things were starting to make sense.

Ms. Lowery turned on her computer and then printed out a transcript showing Jada's grades up until that point in the school year. Two months into the school year Jada had a 2.0 GPA.

"As you can see Mr. Simms Jada is barely passing her classes."

"Yes I can see. Is there any way you can have Jada come here?"

Ms. Lowery called the classroom Jada was in at the time and instructed the teacher to send her to the office. When Jada opened the door to Ms. Lowery's office she looked as if she'd seen a ghost. I was the last person she expected to see.

"Jada I called you here because your father has informed me that your mother didn't die."

"I never said my mother died!" Jada responded in a shaky tone – the look of guilt was all over her face.

"Jada, one of your classmates came to me crying and said that you were contemplating committing suicide – is that true."

Jada just sat there staring at the floor. I couldn't contain my anger.

"Don't just sit there looking silly – answer the lady!" I yelled. My tone caused Ms. Lowery to jump back in her seat and tears to role down Jada's cheeks.

For about ten seconds the office was eerily quiet. My anger wouldn't let it stay that way.

"Let me first say to you Ms. Lowery that I apologize to you for having to deal with this fantastic lie. Unfortunately, Jada has a propensity to do and say anything to detract attention from her downfalls. It appears to me that she has chosen to make up this story and use it as the reason she's been performing poorly in school. I can assure you that her grades will improve and that there will be no more lies."

I looked at Jada the entire time I spoke to Ms. Lowery. Tears were flowing down her face like Niagara Falls. I stood up and shook Ms. Lowery's hand and than exited the office. Before I could make it to my car in the parking lot I'd already called Dawn from my cell phone to tell her what happened.

"Jamal I know you're pissed and you should be, but I think you may be missing the bigger picture."

"What bigger picture Dawn? The only picture I see is that this child is just like her fucking mama! You don't know how close I came to slapping the taste out of her mouth right there in front of that white lady!"

"I feel you baby, and don't get me wrong – I believe she is very lazy when it comes to school work. But, I also believe that her making up a story about Tracy dying is some type of cry for help. I think you need to figure out a way to get in touch with Tracy. It's obvious that she and Jada need to talk."

I left the school and went to a nearby bar to have a drink. As I sat there nursing a rum and coke – I thought about Dawn's comments. Maybe she was right. Maybe this shit is deeper than I first thought. I didn't know what to do.

The next day I called Tracy's old job and talked to her former coworker. I told the lady that I had an emergency and I needed her to relay a message to Tracy. Two days later Tracy called and inquired about Jada – it was the first time I'd heard Tracy's voice since she'd promised to pay Jada's tuition bill six months earlier.

"Jamal what's wrong?"

I thought about saying, *You're what's wrong*, but I held back. I decided to chastise her some other time – Jada's situation was more important. I proceeded to tell Tracy what Jada had told the counselor and explained why I felt she needed to reach out to Jada. After I made the suggestion the irony of the situation hit me – I was encouraging Tracy to talk to Jada, and just a few years earlier Tracy was telling me that she'd never try to encourage a relationship between Jada and me.

Tracy called my house later on that night and asked to speak to Jada. Dawn answered the phone. I could tell she was itching to tell Tracy off, but she didn't. She did the next best thing – she threw the phone on the counter - the clanging sound had to have hurt Tracy's ears.

Tracy and Jada talked on the phone for two straight hours. When Jada hung up she seemed like a totally different child. I thought to myself:

Ain't this a bitch! Her mama dissed her for six months – makes one phone call and everything is forgotten. I'll be damned!

The mood in my house was noticeably different during the next few days. Jada was spending more time talking to Dawn and me than she had the entire time she lived with us. As much as I hated to admit it, Tracy's phone call helped. Since the initial contact they'd been talking twice a day.

I still wanted to question Tracy about the tuition bill, but I was hesitant because I didn't want to destroy the positive atmosphere. I figured that Tracy would go back underground if I confronted her, and that would upset Jada.

Two days later, Murphy's Law kicked in. I didn't have to change the atmosphere – Jada was capable of doing that on her own.

One day Dawn came home from work and found a notebook on the kitchen table. The notebook's front cover was nicely decorated, and although she quickly realized that it belonged to Jada, curiosity got the best of her so she opened it. Much to Dawn's surprise - Jada's embarrassment – and my disappointment, the folder contained more offensive language than a N.W.A. rap song.

Inside the folder were letters from several
girls...including Jada. Apparently, it was common
practice at her high school for a group of girls to share
a diary. The diary (in this case a spiral notebook)
would be passed around from girl to girl, and they
wrote comments about anything and everyone. Most of
Jada's comments in the notebook were about her
"enemies" and boys she lusted after. Jada's comments
were very graphic and disturbing, but despite how
disappointed Dawn was with Jada – she was prepared
to chalk it up to teenage immaturity. Dawn was about
to close the notebook when she noticed that on one
page Jada made a few snide remarks about us:

*My daddy and step mama get on my fucking nerves! I
can't stand them! They told me they're gonna think
about letting me go to the dance. I'm going even if I
gotta sneak out. Fuck them – they can't control me! I
can't wait to get out of this fucking house!*

Dawn begin to compare Jada's remarks with those
of the other girls and noticed that no one else talked
about their parents. Their remarks about sex were
equally crass, but none of the other girls made any
references to their parents.
When I came home Dawn wasted little time
showing me the notebook.
"She has got to go!"
"What are you talkin' bout?"
"Read this shit," Dawn replied and threw the
notebook at me.
I'd never seen her this way. She was usually the
voice of reason when it came to dealing with Jada –
now she looked as if she wanted to kill the child.
I read the notebook and immediately felt like
punching a hole in the wall. I knew Jada was no
angel, but I never thought she could be this vulgar or
talk about Dawn and me in such a negative way.

As I entered Jada's bedroom carrying the notebook my heart sank because I knew what I had to do. I threw the notebook on Jada's bed.

"Is that what you think of us?" I asked.

"I didn't mean anything by what I said. Why were ya'll reading my stuff anyway?" Jada nervously replied.

I closed Jada's bedroom door and commenced to giving her the most intense verbal ass chewing I'd ever given her.

"We read your stuff because you left that trash on the kitchen table out in the open where anyone could read it...including your little brother! After all the sacrifices we've made for you this is how you repay us...by calling us names?"

Jada became silent, but the look on her face spoke volumes...no remorse, no sorrow, and she seemed more annoyed at the fact that she had been busted than concerned about the people she'd hurt. It was at that point that I knew that Jada was not only a replica of Tracy in looks, but she possessed the same self-centered inability to accept responsibility for her actions as Tracy.

My anger grew to the point that I punched the wall so hard I nearly put a hole in it. I could feel my eyes getting watery, and an uncomfortable knot grew in my throat. I watched as Jada just sat there with her usual blank stare. Her lack of concern pushed me over the edge.

"I give up! You have approximately thirty days after your graduation to get out of my house - so I suggest you start making your plans now."

As I closed Jada's door and walked away I could feel the tears rolling down my face. For the first time during my daughter's 17 years of existence, I had given up on her. I spent the next four hours replaying scenes from her life and pondering aloud whether I had done everything I was supposed to do as a father:

Did I spend enough time with her? Did I do enough to help build up her self-esteem? Was Jada's lack of drive and motivation a genetic trait or was it learned behavior? How will we all co-exist in the same house during the remainder of the school year?

In the midst of this pensive moment one thing became clear to me...my relationship with Jada would never be the same again. Suddenly, those dark memories that I'd learned to suppress resurfaced. I started thinking about the day I was given that paperwork at the child support office years earlier. I became fixated with the fact that Jada had not inherited any of my physical features or personality traits. It was as if this incident caused me to notice things I chose to ignore for years - like her aloof behavior and lack of affection towards me. The paternity question that had been lurking in the back of my mind for seventeen years needed to be answered. As I sat in my office smoking my last cigarette I contemplated my next move.

Trying to be noble isn't always easy. For years I had kept my feelings on the back burner, and ignored the urge to confront Tracy about the document I had received from the child support office years earlier. After hours of contemplation I decided to seek the closure I so desperately needed.

Jada's eighteenth birthday was only a few weeks away so I didn't have much time left. Once she turned eighteen years old she would be considered an adult, and she'd have to consent to the test. I wasn't about to let this opportunity slip away - I made arrangements to have a DNA test performed.

My desire to know the truth didn't totally cloud my judgment – I tried to be as covert as possible. In an effort to avoid traumatizing Jada during her senior year of school, I decided to make up a reason for having the test done. I decided to tell her that the test was being conducted in conjunction with a new life insurance policy I'd purchased on her. Jada's initial response was interesting to say the least.

"Why I gotta have a test...I'm your child!" she blurted out as she looked at me quizzically.

Jada's comment left me speechless. I looked over at Dawn for support, but that was a waste of time – she just stood there in shock with her mouth wide open and then stepped into the laundry room to get out of Jada's sight. I was left standing in the kitchen looking like a damn fool. After a few seconds of awkward silence I responded.

"Girl this ain't got nuthin' to do with you being my child. This is a big insurance policy - it's standard that we take this kind of test. They wanna make sure you ain't got some kind of pre-existing disease or anything."

I felt like an awe struck contestant on Showtime at the Apollo. I wanted to be escorted out of the room by the Sandman. But, since the Sandman nor Kiki Sheppard were nowhere in site, I did the next best thing - I backpedaled into the laundry room.

Dawn was leaning on the washing machine laughing her ass off.

"That shit ain't funny! Why you gonna leave me out there hangin'?" I whispered trying to contain my own laughter.

Dawn gestured for me to lower my voice, and took a moment to wipe the tears from her eyes. "That was funny. You looked more nervous than a hooker in church," she finally replied.

"Girl pull yourself together – you got slob and shit hangin' from your chin! She's gonna be lookin' at us when we walk outta here so you gotta be cool – stop laughing!"

When we walked out Jada was staring right at us. I didn't bother to look her way – I just headed straight for the steps. Dawn hid her face behind a basket of unfolded clothes she'd taken from the laundry room as she followed me up the stairs.

The magnitude of this situation was beginning to weigh heavily on my spirit. I felt a type of nervousness that I'd never felt before. On top of the realization that I was gonna know the answer to a decade old question – I had to be very mindful of who I was dealing with. Tracy's ass was crazy – I needed to be absolutely sure of the DNA results.

To eliminate the possibility of Tracy denouncing the results, I avoided anything that remotely resembled any type of home kit. One day, after watching a talk show that focused on DNA testing, I paid close attention as the credits scrolled at the end of the show. I grabbed an ink pen and jotted down the name and phone number of the company that performed the DNA test for the talk show. The very next day I called to get more information on how the test was conducted. Much to my surprise, the company that conducted the test had a service agreement with several hospitals within 50 miles of my zip code. Within five minutes the representative and I had agreed on a hospital lab and exam date.

The DNA test cost $600 – which was actually a bargain; it would have cost more if I had paid to get the test results in three days. Getting the results back in three days was of no importance to me, hell, I'd already waited seventeen years so two more weeks wouldn't hurt me.

The testing company's representative wrote down my zip code and searched their database to see if an authorized testing hospital was nearby. We were sent to a hospital located approximately thirty minutes from my house.

When the day of the test came I was so scared that I thought about canceling. Dawn tried to tell me that I'd waited long enough to know the truth, and that I had a right to know; she also reminded me that the $600 was non-refundable.

As Jada and I wandered aimlessly around the hospital looking for the laboratory, the mood was comparable to attending a funeral. Neither of us said much. It was as if she instinctively knew that there was more to this situation than I was telling her.

Finally, I told Jada to sit in the lobby while I sought out some directions. A few minutes later I found the laboratory and went inside to explain the situation to the lab technician. I told her that Jada was unaware of the reasoning for the DNA test; therefore, it was imperative that they avoid making any comments regarding paternity.

Jada walked into the lab and sat down quietly. The sterile smell of the room was disturbing. It was the kind of room that screamed "something's wrong". Jada looked around at the dull pictures on the wall, and was literally shaking from anxiety about what was transpiring. At that moment, she didn't seem like a rebellious 17-year-old. The look on her face reminded me of the innocent child in the restaurant screaming at me to watch her while she played; the beautiful child that always insisted that I stay awake during those boring animated movies. This was my baby – the child I'd helped nurture. A part of me wanted to grab her by the arm and leave, but I knew that I'd be doing myself an injustice. I had to bring closure to this paternity issue once and for all – for my own sanity.

The lab technician administered the oral swab test, and was finished within five minutes. I'd pulled it off – Jada didn't know what was going on – I'd protected her from the potentially devastating truth. Still, the thought of lying to her made me feel sleazy and uncomfortable. I wanted to tell her the truth, but my job as her father was to protect her for as long as I could. I vowed to myself that if the results were negative I wouldn't tell Jada until after she graduated from high school.

As we walked back to the car I gave Jada a hug and kissed her on the forehead. I wondered if I'd made the right decision. For years, I'd always placed her needs and wants ahead of my own, but this time I'd placed my own needs first. As I watched Jada get into the car a heartbreaking feeling came over me...suddenly, having the DNA test conducted wasn't as liberating and gratifying as I envisioned it would be. Regrettably, there was no turning back at this point...Pandora's Box had been opened.

Two weeks into my wait for the DNA results, any attempts to focus on work or my family were an exercise in futility. I was so nervous that I was regretting not having paid the extra $100 for the three-day results. Only a death row inmate making his way towards the gas chamber could describe a more agonizing journey than the one I embarked upon the day I went to the post office. My hands shook uncontrollably and made it hard for me to insert the key and open up the post office box. I stared at the gold envelope inside the box for seconds before I pulled it out. I'm sure I looked more nervous than a man handling a package of explosives.

For some strange reason I started clearing my throat the way you do when you're about to speak. It must have been some type of anxious reflex because I wasn't about to say anything to anyone. The last time I'd felt more nervous about a letter was during my eight-grade year in junior high school when I rushed home to intercept one of my many sub-par report cards.

I wasn't going to open up the most important piece of mail I'd ever received in front of a bunch of strangers, so I took the letter to my car. The wind was strong that evening, but I wasn't going to let Mother Nature pry this potentially life-changing envelope from my grasp. If there were such a thing as a DNA bandit on the prowl snatching DNA test results out of the hands of unsuspecting brotha's, his ass would have caught a monumental beat down on this particular day.

As I sat in my car trying to regain my composure, I looked out of my front, back, rear view, and side windows to make sure no one was peaking in trying to see my test results. I even looked in the back seat just to be sure the DNA bandit wouldn't sneak up on me – I didn't need anyone distracting me once I cast my watery eyes on the test results. Finally, I took one last deep breath and said a brief prayer:

GOD please give me the strength to handle these results if they reveal that I'm not Jada's father.

Having spoken to my GOD, I suddenly felt confidant I could handle anything so I opened the envelope and read the results. Discreetly nestled amidst lines and lines of unnecessary wording lay the sentence I was looking for, *"The probability that the alleged father (Jamal L. Simms) is the biological father of Jada P. Simms is 0%."*

My eyes veered away and then I looked at the letter again - squinting like a partially blind man as I read the results. I figured that my eyes had deceived me, but they hadn't. I read the results a third time aloud, as if that would change their meaning. The radio had been playing during the entire time I sat there, but I'd totally tuned out the music as I read the document. I had the focus of an NBA player trying to concentrate on shooting foul shots at the end of a game. I read the document a fourth time just to be sure of the results. After reading the words aloud for a final time I allowed the paper to fall to my lap. Suddenly, the music in my car became audible and I could hear the sultry voice of Anita Baker as she sang the words to her classic song "Angel":

If I could I'd give you the wooooorld, wrap it all around you; won't be satisfied with just a piece of his heart – my Annnnnnnngel.

The words didn't help my emotional state. Before I knew it, twenty minutes elapsed while I leaned forward in my seat with my head resting on the steering wheel – crying my eyes out. The tears became uncontrollable, and although I knew there was a possibility someone would see me in this helpless state, I simply could not muster up the strength to regain my self-control.

Just as I was beginning to read the results for a fifth time, an elderly lady knocked on my passenger side window, "Baby are you okay?" she asked.

I quickly rolled down the window and replied, "Yes maam." The tears streaming down my face contradicted my every word.

"Sweetheart I don't know what you're going through, but you need to know that trouble doesn't last always...you gonna be alright! GOD doesn't place any more on us than we can handle," the lady said as she slowly turned and walked away.

The mysterious lady's words were just as piercing to my soul as the DNA test results had been. I started crying again. As my tears subsided and I slowly became more aware of my surroundings, I realized that being an emotional wreck in public was probably an ugly sight. My hands trembled ferociously as I fought to place the letter back inside of the envelope.

I drove home in a daze. I can remember being flipped the "bird" by at least three different drivers as my car straddled the centerline and occasionally swerved into their lane. I couldn't see straight. I couldn't think straight. My mind struggled to comprehend the harsh reality that had landed in my lap – literally.

"I'm not Jada's father," I mumbled. I'd cried so much that the mucous in my nose clogged my nostrils and made it hard for me to breath. I pulled my car to the side of the road, and blew my nose until the only thing remaining was my nose hairs. I could feel my temple pulsate as the mother of all migraines kicked in.

I sat in my car on the side of the road for a few minutes and stared at joggers who looked too frail to be jogging and walkers that were so overweight they should have been jogging. Suddenly, the heartbreak I felt subsided. The tears dried up and were replaced by thoughts of rage. I became angry – no I got pissed. All I could think about at that point was Tracy. To be more accurate, all I could think about was what I was going to do to Tracy when I saw her.

I continued my drive home and started to reminisce about the seventeen years of stress I'd endured as a result of the lie Tracy told when she called my house in 1986. One by one the scenes kept flashing across my mind:

The first day I sat in the recruiters office and made plans to join the army so that I could take care of the child I thought was mine; all the times Tracy changed her phone number and address and wouldn't let me see Jada; the day I saw pictures of Jada and Mannie at the prison; the time Tracy told me I wasn't going to amount to shit - just like my dad; the time I took the money for my car payment and purchased a plane ticket for Jada, only to have the ticket go to waste because Tracy failed to put the child on the plane; the time she told me that she would never encourage a relationship between Jada and I; the time she flipped me the "bird" and told me to "just send the fucking child support check"; the fact that I upset Dawn by cashing out my son's college fund to clear Tracy's debt with the school....

The more I thought about the past, the more incidents kept coming to my mind. Memories about incidents I hadn't thought about in years. I begin to question every decision Tracy made over the years, wondering if her motives had something to do with this lie:

Maybe that's why she never wanted Jada to come live with me when the child was failing in school – it had nothing to do with grades – it was because she knew deep down that Jada wasn't my child. No mother would let her child go live with a man who isn't the biological father.

When I arrived at my home I felt like a complete idiot for making the sacrifices I'd made over the years. I sat in my car in my driveway thinking about my next move. I was angry and I wanted revenge for the way I'd been bamboozled. Since opening the test results, I'd felt nothing but contempt for Tracy. I wanted to hurt her in a way that made her feel as debilitated as I was feeling.

Suddenly, a thought crossed my mind that I had never really considered before...has Jada known the entire time? The first thing that came out of Jada's mouth when she learned of the test was, *"Why I gotta have a test...I'm your child!"*

I replayed the events that led up to my decision to get the DNA test. I also thought about my relationship with Jada over the years.

Once again, my mind started to drift:

Why did she say that? Why would she assume that the test was a paternity test? For years it was difficult to get close to Jada – getting her to show affection and appreciation was like trying to read Mandarin Chinese. Was it the lack of a genetic connection that made it difficult to bond?

I was driving myself crazy. I didn't tell Dawn about the test results when I went inside. I placed the envelope on my office desk, put in my "Best of Sade" CD, and collapsed on the plush leather sofa in my office. I spent the next few hours in that spot looking up at the ceiling. Before I knew it, the tears that ran down both sides of my face had created little puddles on the sofa on each side of my head. I wiped away my tears, closed my eyes, and tried to pretend that the entire day was just one bad dream.

I awakened the next morning ready to go to war. I spent the entire day plotting my next move. I left no stone unturned, and by the end of the day I had outlined a course of action that rivaled any business plan I'd ever created. Although Jada's emotional well being remained paramount, I still felt used, humiliated, and angry; making Tracy suffer for her scandalous behavior was at the top of my priority list.

Christmas was a few weeks away. My family and I were returning to New Orleans for the holidays so I decided to wait until the day after Christmas to tell Tracy about the test. Still, there was one last issue I needed to address - I needed someone to witness the conversation.

Haphazardly choosing a witness was not in my plans; I knew that the witness needed to be someone whom Tracy held in high regard and was trying to impress. After careful deliberation I decided to avoid Tracy's family, and confront Tracy in front of the person whom I felt she wanted to impress the most...her fiancé Samuel.

Now that I had decided on my approach, and my witness, all I needed was the location. During an earlier conversation Jada had mentioned that Tracy and her fiancée would be doing their Christmas shopping at the Promenade Mall that weekend. This was perfect for me because all I needed to do was set the stage.

I called Tracy a few days before Christmas to put my plan in motion. I'd been in town for a day or so, and had already scouted the mall. I couldn't remember the last time I was this eager to call Tracy. At approximately nine o'clock in the morning I called Tracy and told her I wouldn't be able to shop for Jada's gift. I asked Tracy if I could meet her in the mall, and give her some money to purchase Jada's gift on my behalf. To ensure she wouldn't balk at the idea, I decided to use Tracy's own greed to seal the deal. I told her that I'd slip her $100 to buy herself something...she took the bait.

We made plans to meet in the mall's food court at noon. I knew that the element of surprise was essential if I was to have my victory - calling this a victory was a stretch, but it sure beat choking the shit out of her.

Now that the stage was set, all that remained was choosing my delivery. As Tracy and Samuel approached, I felt like scrapping my plan to confront her in a civil manner and grabbing her weave (which had miraculously grown 6 inches since I'd last seen her). She was grinning from ear to ear as she flaunted him in front of me.

Samuel was a 6'6" former college basketball star, with dreams of being a NBA star. Unfortunately, like thousands of other 6'6" former basketball stars with dreams of signing a shoe contract, he was finding out that you have to be more than just good to make it into the NBA...you have to be damn good!

While he waited for his next big tryout, Tracy's fiancée spent his days as a bouncer in a local nightclub. Tracy was totally enamored with the prospect that this guy could one day be the "next big thing"; therefore, she was determined to latch on to this man and his wallet...by any means necessary.

I sat in the food court trying to eat a hamburger when Tracy approached me. She blatantly flashed what looked like a 1 or 2-carat diamond ring. The closer she got the more I could see that the diamond was as phony as the hair she was wearing.

"Hi Jamal, this is Samuel. Samuel, this is my baby daddy."

Samuel and I gave each other the - *I don't really want to meet this nigga* - head nod.

"Looks like you've been doin' some shoppin' already. What you got in the bags?" she asked.

"Nothing special, but I do have something here for you." I replied with a smile.

I reached inside of the bag and pulled out the DNA test results.

"What's this?" she asked as she opened the envelope.

"Oh it's just the results of a DNA test that I had done."

"What?"

"You heard me. As you can clearly see, the test revealed that Jada is not my child."

Tracy looked as if she had been kicked in the stomach by a mule. I couldn't tell if the stupid look on her face was the byproduct of stomach cramps resulting from something she ate or shock that I had discovered her little secret.

She looked back at her Samuel in disbelief. I took the results from her, and read the test results. I then glanced at Samuel and gave him the test results. Samuel read the test results and then looked at Tracy like she was the scum of the earth, "Looks like you owe this man an explanation," he remarked.

Tracy panicked. She didn't know what to say. Finally she started yelling at me.

"I can't believe you brought me here for this shit! What are you talking about she's not your child? Where are you getting this shit?" she screamed.

The food court that was once bustling with activity instantly became quiet.

"I don't know why you are so shocked - the results don't lie. You were obviously fucking someone else and gave me the charge. By the way, you need to close your mouth before you let a fly in," I said with a smirk.

"I don't believe the test is true. I wasn't there, and I don't know where you got those results. Besides, why would you wait all these years to have a paternity test done?" she asked.

"I thought you'd never ask," I replied as I sat down at the table. "I have here in my possession a document that you signed roughly 13 years ago. The document comes from the child support office. As you can see, you clearly indicated that during the time of conception you were sleeping with someone else. I never showed you this because I didn't think it was appropriate to confuse Jada at the time - she was still so young. Also, I didn't want to give you an excuse to accuse me of attempting to get out of paying child support; therefore, I chose to wait until she was eighteen years old before I had a paternity test. Now I got the test, and your ass is busted."

Tracy's eyes got bigger and her lips begin to quiver. She looked totally confused. Her fiancé had a stunned look on his face. As she continued to stand there looking stupid, I stared at her with repulsion and shook my head. I looked to my left and saw a young couple eating popcorn and looking at us like they were watching a movie. Normally I would have told them to mind their business, but this time I didn't care. I wanted everyone to know how scandalous Tracy was.

Tracy was exposed and she knew it. She did the only thing she could at that point...she started crying.

"Jamal, I wasn't with anyone else!" she yelled. "I want a second test done, and I want to be involved in the process."

'That's fine; I don't give a shit how many tests you get done because I ain't paying for it. Besides, this test is all the proof I need because now I know the truth. You say you weren't with anyone else, but one thing is true, I didn't get you pregnant. So, I guess you must be the Virgin Mary. You can keep that copy of the paternity test because I have plenty more at home. You have until the end of this school year to do whatever it is you're going to do. That gives you about four or five months to tell the truth before I do what I have to do," I said as I took one last bite of my hamburger.

"What does that mean?" Tracy asked as she searched for a tissue to wipe the mascara that was starting to run down her face.

"You don't come clean by the end of this school year, and you're gonna find out what I mean. By the way, I haven't told Jada because I wanted to talk to you first. I don't believe she should have to deal with something this heavy during her senior year of school. That's why I'm prepared to wait until after her graduation before I take this to another level. I want her to return to Texas with me, and complete her senior year. Right now her grades are the best they've ever been – she has a "B" average. She's doing well and I don't want to disrupt that. Are we in agreement?"

Tracy shook her head in agreement as tears continued to roll down her face. I left Tracy and Samuel standing there in the center of the food court. It was the first time in eighteen years that I had an argument with Tracy that I felt I'd actually won. From the moment I obtained the document from the child support office I'd visualized this confrontation and Tracy's subsequent reaction. For years I'd envisioned a long drawn out argument, but it didn't happen that way. The entire verbal exchange lasted less than five minutes.

I walked calmly out of the mall and waited until I got into the parking lot before I let out a scream that was so loud it caused one passersby to look at me as if I were some kind of a lunatic. I didn't care - it felt as if the weight of the world had been lifted off of my shoulders. It didn't take away the hurt, but if only for a moment, I felt vindicated.

Tracy

When Jamal confronted me in the mall that day I didn't know how to respond. I was shocked, embarrassed, and confused. I couldn't believe he'd done something like that in such a public place. My fiancé was looking at me like I was some type of a slut.

Later that night, I sat in my bedroom and started crying for what seemed like hours. I called Jamal to try to ask him why he'd embarrassed me like that...and why he felt the need to do it in front of my man. Jamal wouldn't let me get a word in; he cursed me for ten straight minutes. He didn't stop cursing until I asked him one question...why did he wait eighteen years to get a DNA test if he'd always felt Jada may not have been his child? When I asked him that he just paused – he didn't really have an answer.

Jamal is a smart man – I just don't believe he would have waited eighteen years to get a DNA test if he felt I was lying. I remember he said that he was trying to put his desire to know the truth on the backburner and focus on Jada. But, I wish he would have had a DNA test done earlier in her life rather than allow her to get attached to him all those years and then drop a bomb like that on her.

I still don't know what his motives were. Maybe he was mad at her for something she did. Maybe he was mad at me for some of the decisions I'd made in the past – I don't know. One thing is for sure - he traumatized my child.

I called my girlfriend Lala after I hung up the phone, and asked her to come over so we could talk. I've known Lala since I was in the seventh grade. She knew everything about me; most of the ripping and running I did as a child, I did with her. We sat up all night trying to remember if I'd been with someone else.

"Tracy, I don't know what Jamal was thinking about when he did this. Doesn't he realize how this could impact Jada's emotional state?"

"Girl, I don't know why he had this test done. I don't even know if the test is legitimate – I wasn't there."

"That's true – you don't know where he had this test done."

"I think this is the most selfish thing he has ever done. He's been in her life all these years, and now he wants to start this shit. He still can't explain why he felt the need to do it."

"If I were you, I wouldn't even worry about it."

"How can I not worry about it Lala? Now I have to explain to Jada why her daddy is questioning whether she's his daughter."

"You don't have to try to explain anything – he's gonna have to explain his actions to Jada. You know you weren't sleeping with anyone else so don't worry about it. He's probably jealous that you are going to marry Samuel. Jamal just can't stand to see you happy."

"Lala, I don't know what to do."

"I just told you what to do – nothing. The burden of proof is on him – not you."

"I gotta talk to Jada. She's going back to Texas with Jamal and I don't know what he's going to say about me."

"You're right, he's gonna have a lot of time to poison her mind. You definitely need to tell her your side of what happened because you may not get another chance."

It was at that moment I decided to talk to Jada and tell her everything that happened. My child just sat there with a stunned look on her face. Jada doesn't cry easily, but I can tell when she's upset. She went into my bedroom to lay in my bed. I crawled in the bed with her – I've never seen my child cry so hard. She was devastated – Jamal really hurt her.

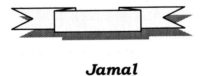

Jamal

Tracy called me on the phone that night, crying and saying she was sorry. For nearly ten minutes I gave her a verbal tongue-lashing.

I don't remember everything that was said that night, but I do remember that she kept asking me why I'd waited eighteen years to have the DNA test done. At first I was stomped by her question – I knew why I'd waited – I was trying to protect Jada. But, in true Tracy fashion, she'd figured out a way to shift the blame.

"Why did you wait so long?" Tracy asked.

"Why does it matter?"

"Jamal, it matters because you and Jada have developed a bond, and now you've got her confused."

"Bullshit! The only that's confusing is your story. The fact that I waited eighteen years is irrelevant – what's important is the fact that you lied to her and me. I did what I did because I felt it was in Jada's best interest to wait, but I've always planned on finding out the truth. Whether I waited eighteen years or eight years is not as important as the fact that you've been hiding the truth. How about we talk about that...the truth! Who is Jada's real father?"

Tracy started crying again. I guess she thought I was going to feel sorry for her ass, but I didn't.

"Look Tracy, I don't want to hear you crying in my damn ear. All I want to hear is you telling the truth. Call me when you are ready to stop lying. Tell Jada to pack her bags – we're going back to Texas in the morning."

I hung up the phone and spent the rest of that night loading up my bags. The next morning I went to Tracy's house to pick-up Jada on my way out of town. As I pulled up I could see Jada standing outside crying. I immediately knew that my biggest fears had come true...Tracy had already told Jada about the paternity test.

In typical Tracy fashion she disregarded the potential negative emotional ramifications this news would have on a child already struggling to make it through her senior year of high school. Her only goal was to get "her" side of the story out first. I never had much trust in anything Tracy said, but I honestly believed she would honor our agreement to keep the results secret until after Jada graduated from high school...I was wrong.

Jada

My dad wanted to talk about the DNA test results, but to be honest with you – I didn't want to be bothered. All I wanted to do was just crawl up in my bed, go to sleep, and make everything go away. Unfortunately, it wasn't that easy.

I had mixed emotions about the test results. On one hand I believed them and knew that my mama must have been cheating on my daddy years ago. On the other hand, I was mad at my daddy for getting the test done in the first place. He'd been my daddy all those years and all of a sudden he wanted to have a test done. I knew something was wrong when he took me to that hospital – I never thought he would lie to me.

He kept asking me if I felt like my mother owed me an explanation. I told him maybe, but I didn't care about the test results. As far as I was concerned he was my real daddy. He kept telling me that it did matter, and that my mama had lied to both of us. I knew he was right, but I didn't want to hear that. I felt like he was trying to disown me. I still don't understand why he had to go and get the test.

I can remember how awkward it felt during that week. Dawn hardly said a word to me. She wasn't mean to me, but it was obvious that something had changed. I felt like the walls were closing in on me. To be honest with you, I had so much fun in New Orleans during the holidays that I didn't really want to go back to Texas. If it weren't for the fact that I still had a few months left in school – I would have asked if I could stay.

From that point on, I just never looked at him the same way.

Jamal

Jada and I discussed the test results and agreed that her mother owed both of us an explanation.

It had been three days since I confronted her mom, and both Jada and I were waiting for Tracy to call and offer an explanation. We were also waiting for instructions on when and where to take the second DNA test...or so I thought.

Tracy called me on the fourth day and attempted once again to explain the results of the paternity test. She told me that she was prepared to accept the results of my DNA test, but she still couldn't remember having sex with anyone else. I was not impressed with her attempt at an apology. In my opinion, Tracy seemed very insincere and uncertain. The anger I felt made it easy for me to express my sentiments to her. Eventually I told her to work on her story more because she would need to be more convincing when she spoke to Jada.

"I've already talked to Jada," Tracy responded.

"What do you mean you've talked to Jada?"

"I've spoken to Jada by phone and e-mail on three different occasions since ya'll returned to Texas. Jada was satisfied with my explanation, and wants to move on with her life. She doesn't want any other man to provide for her," Tracy said.

"So what – I'm supposed to be flattered by that?" I asked in a stern tone. "You know, I'm glad you brought up the issue of providing support. Now that we know I'm not Jada's biological father, we need to discuss the issue of support. I've provided for her financially for 18 years. As a matter of fact, I've never asked you for any type of financial assistance even when she has lived with me."

Tracy just held the phone – no response, not even a peep out of her. Her guilt was so apparent that if it was liquid it would have oozed through the phone line.

"Now that Jada is about to graduate high school – who is going to pay for her to go to college? Who is going to buy her a car? Are you prepared to finance all of these big ticket expenses?" I asked.

"Well Jamal, you said that you were going to buy her a car and pay for her to go to college. I think you should do what you said you were gonna do," she responded.

"What!" I yelled. "Have you lost your fucking mind? Do you really expect me to pay thousands of dollars for a car and college tuition for a child that I know isn't mind. You don't even have enough respect for me to tell me who the real father is. Do you honestly think I'm gonna spend more of my hard earned money? Ya'll contacting each other like nothing ever happened – I think both of ya'll trying to "play" me."

I paused for a moment to catch my breath. I was so angry that I could feel a weird sensation shoot up and down my spine.

"Not only are you ungrateful and selfish, you are the biggest user I've ever met. Well, you've used me for damn near two decades – the bank is closed! I suggest you contact her real daddy, and ask that mutha fucka to pay for his child. As far as I'm concerned, he had an 18 year break - now it's time for him to start digging into his pockets."

I slammed the phone on the receiver. My hands were shaking – I was floored. Dawn heard me yelling and came into the room. When I told her that Tracy refused to talk about the test results, but expected me to continue to provide financial support for Jada she yelled, "Bullshit!"

I was extremely disappointed and annoyed at the fact that Tracy and Jada had been talking to each other for three days without me knowing. I was also disgusted with Jada because I felt that her reluctance to deal with this issue, and her eagerness to "sweep it under the rug" alleviated Tracy of her responsibility to tell the truth about this eighteen-year-old lie.

I decided that I wouldn't tell Jada I'd spoken to her mom because I wanted to see if she would inform me that she'd spoken to her mother.

Days passed and I became more frustrated whenever Jada failed to take advantage of an opportunity to tell me that she'd spoken to her mother. I viewed her reluctance to deal with the issue as a sign of weakness. I knew that Jada's current behavior was consistent with the way she'd dealt with other problems, but that didn't lessen my frustration.

I felt that she should have been more vocal and frustrated with her mom. I didn't expect her to sever all ties with Tracy, but I did feel that she should've demanded answers from Tracy...if not for herself; she should've demanded answers on my behalf.

My frustration reached its apex the following week when I heard Jada laughing while speaking to Tracy on the phone. As far as I was concerned Jada was conversing with the enemy, and I couldn't stand it. As soon as she hung up the phone I confronted her.

"You and your mama seem to be getting along well."

"Yeah, she was telling me about her day at work."

"Has she told you anything about your biological father?" I asked.

"No. She didn't bring it up, and to be honest with you - I don't want to know." Jada responded nonchalantly.

"What do you mean you don't want to know? Your mom has been misleading both of us for eighteen years; she owes both of us an explanation," I yelled.

"You expect me to be mad forever?" Jada responded.

"No, but I expect you to be mad for longer than a week. I expect you to be mad for me. It hasn't been two weeks, and you're already letting her off the hook. What about me? I worked my ass off trying to take care of you - I deserve some answers. You're damn right I believe you should be mad...you owe me that."

Jada started crying and ran out of the living room towards her bedroom. Dawn came up stairs to see what was wrong, and when she saw my disposition she quickly grabbed me by the arm and led me into our bedroom.

Dawn commenced to rub my shoulders as I sat on the edge of our bed. My shoulder muscles were so tight they felt like bricks. I was beginning to wonder if I'd made a mistake bringing Jada home with me. I was trying to do the noble thing by letting Jada return to live with me for the remainder of the school year, but now I wasn't sure if that was such a good idea. Every time I looked at Jada I saw Tracy; furthermore, I saw an 18 year-old young adult that was incapable of standing up for what was right.

I begin to wonder if the migraine headaches, which I knew could be linked to my high blood pressure, were my body's way of telling me that this situation was more than I could handle.

There were still five months remaining in the school year, and I didn't know what to do. I felt used by Tracy and betrayed by Jada. My health was beginning to take a turn for the worse, and with each passing day it was becoming more and more apparent that no one in my immediate circle could completely understand how much the results of the paternity test had devastated me.

The next morning I sat Jada down and explained my position to her. As I fought to hold back tears I looked into her eyes and said what was on my mind.

"Jada I want you to know that I truly love you, and I will always be here for you if you need me; however, I realize that you will never be as angry with your mother as I am, and I have a problem accepting that. I don't expect you to stop having a relationship with your mother, and I would never try to encourage you to cut her out of your life. But, she has hurt me, and although you may be willing to forgive her - I can't right now. I also can't handle her calling here two and three times a day, and the two of you laughing and talking on the phone as if the DNA results don't exist. Your mama lied for eighteen years, and I can't pretend that didn't happen. In order for me to get over this I need her out of my life. As long as she continues to call here, and refuses to tell me the truth about what happened I can't move on. Dawn and I have talked, and we both agree that maybe the best place for you is back in New Orleans with your mother."

Dawn

Wanda's instincts must have been on overdrive because her phone call could not have come at a better time. We hadn't talked to each other in over a month – not since that night she was going on her date. I wanted to call her earlier in the week, but I knew that she was in Japan working on some big merger. When I saw her name show up on my cell phone I immediately grabbed the phone and went outside and sat in my car so that I could avoid being heard.

"Wanda!" I screeched. I know that my tone must have startled her, because I surprised myself. "Girl I really need to talk to you. I hope you have at least an hour to spare."

"Baaaby, you know I always have time for you. I'm just sitting here debating on whether or not to go to the movies with Larry."

"I thought you liked Larry? The last time we talked the two of you were watching movies at your house."

"Yeah I know, but I'm losing interest."

"Why?"

"You ain't gonna believe this, but it's his hygiene."

"What! His hygiene? Are you trying to say the man stinks?"

"I ain't sayin' he's funky under the arms, but he got some stinky ass feet!"

"Wanda what are you talkin' about?"

"Girl the last time he was here we were having a good time. We'd been drinking a little wine and I let him rub my shoulders – shit I was startin' to feel good. I was actually thinkin' about giving him some ass, but I had to do the test first."

"Oh no Wanda, not the feet test?"

"Yeah girl I had to check his feet. You know I can't fool with a man who has jacked up feet!"

"So how were his feet?"

"I don't know. I told him to place his feet on my lap so that I can give him a foot massage, and girl I swear I saw a green fog coming from his toes."

"You what?"

"Dawn, this man had the funkiest feet I've ever smelled in my life. I can't tell you how his feet looked because I couldn't get past the smell."

"What did you do?"

"I put his ass out!"

"No you didn't?"

"Girl, I told him to leave and don't come back until he saw a foot specialist or somebody. He called me later apologizing; talkin' about he'd been playing basketball earlier that day. Don't get me wrong, he's cute and got a good job, but Dawn you know how I am – the first time he tries to kiss me all I'll see are those funky ass feet coming towards my face."

I could barely laugh at my friend's story. What I really wanted to do was cry - not for me, but for Jamal.

"Dawn, are you alright."

"Not really – I need to talk you. I paused for a second as the reality of what I was about to say hit me like a ton of bricks. From out of nowhere I was overcome with emotion, and I begin to cry.

Wanda didn't know what was happening, "Dee what's wrong baby? Do you need me to come there? Talk to me!"

I regained my composure and tried to speak clearly, "Wanda everything is going wrong. Jamal had a test done."

"What kind of test? Is he sick?"

"No. He had a DNA test done to make sure Jada was his child."

"He what! Where did this come from?"

"We've always had suspicions, but they were nothing more than suspicions. Since Jada was turning 18 soon, he decided to get the test done since he had custody and she was still a minor. If he had tried to get a test after she turned 18, it would have required Jada's consent."

"Dawn, please don't say what I think you're about to say."

The tears started streaming down my face. This display of emotion was weird for me because up until that point I had been relatively emotionless regarding the topic. Maybe it was because I knew all the time that Jada wasn't Jamal's child. Call it "woman's intuition" or something, but I just knew she wasn't. Still, to see the strongest man I know reduced to tears hurt me deeply.

"Wanda, the test results came back – 0% probability."

"Dawn is there a chance the test was wrong?"

"Wanda, Jamal spent top dollar for this test. The damn thing cost $600 dollars and was done by an actual hospital lab – this wasn't some kind of a home kit. As a matter of fact, he used the same company that those talk shows use to have their paternity test done."

"Oh Dee, I'm so sorry to hear this. I know Jamal must be devastated."

"Wanda I have never seen him like this. Jamal barely cried at his mom's funeral. He locked himself in his office and cried for hours. I don't know what to say or do."

"Does Jada know?"

"Yes she knows – Tracy and Jamal had agreed to wait until after graduation to say something, but Tracy told the child."

"That is one selfish bitch! Rather than worry about the emotional impact that it could have on the child, she was more concerned about getting her side of the story out. Let me guess – she said the test was flawed."

"You know she did. She has convinced that child that she doesn't need to know who her biological father is. She accused Jamal of having the test rigged."

"Rigged? You can't rig a damn DNA test! Does she even know who the real daddy is?"

"Girl I don't know. She swears she wasn't with anyone else at the time."

'That girl is sick. I've read about people like that. She has told that lie for so many years that she's probably starting to believe it herself. But don't fall for it - she knows who the real daddy is...trust me. She may not want to admit it, but she knows. Hell, all women know who they've fucked. I can tell you every piece of dick I've ever had – the good and the bad – the short and the long – the stiff and the limp. However, there is a possibility she was fucking so many people that she doesn't know who the biological father is. Either way, she comes out looking bad."

"Girl, she had the nerve to tell Jamal that he should continue to pay for Jada. She still expects him to buy her a car for graduation, pay for college, and everything else."

"She actually told him that? You know what – I'm not surprised. If he doesn't pay it that means she'll have to come up with the money. Once again, it's not about right or wrong with her – it's about manipulation," said Wanda.

"To make matters worse, Jada and Tracy have been talkin' on the phone like nothing has happened; meanwhile, my husband is in the bedroom crying his fucking eyes out. Girl I wanted to choke the shit out of that little girl."

"Hmmm," Wanda mumbled.

"What's wrong? Why did you say that?"

"Dee, I gotta tell you – if Tracy and Jada are acting like nothing happened than that's pretty damn suspicious to me. I can't help but wonder if Jada may already know who her real daddy is."

"Wanda don't say that."

"I'm just keeping it real with you. The apple doesn't fall far from the tree. Why else wouldn't she be mad with her mama? Sweetheart, nobody's that damn forgiving," said Wanda.

"Wanda, as close as you and your mama are, I know you don't expect me to believe you would stop talking to her after something like this."

"Don't get me wrong - I love my mama to death and there isn't a thing anyone can say to change that. But, just because you love someone doesn't mean you have to be stupid. If my mama had pulled some shit like this, we would have problems until she told the damn truth. I know it's crossed your mind."

"It has crossed my mind, but I have no proof. Even if Jada does know, I don't know when she found out. I don't know if it was during the holidays or did she find out the truth years ago."

"So what are ya'll gonna do now?"

"Jamal told Jada that she had to move back to New Orleans – he just couldn't take her nonchalant attitude about everything."

"Good for him! Neither one of them appreciate him. Jamal doesn't deserve that kind of treatment. I say send her ass back to New Orleans to be with her tired ass mama. They deserve each other – they are two peas in a fucking pod!"

"Wanda I just don't understand how a woman could do that. My conscious wouldn't let me do that to someone. How do you go to church with something like that hanging over your head?"

"Dawn you will never understand because you aren't wired like that. The only people who will sympathize with Tracy are women who have the capacity to do the same thing. As far as going to church - that ain't hard for her. You and I both know that some of the biggest hypocrites you'll ever meet sit in church two and three times a week. That's why they spend so much time preaching to others when they step outside of the church – trying to deflect the attention away from the dirt they do."

I just sat there in silence listening to Wanda. She was so smart and she had a way of cutting to the core of an issue real fast. She was born to be an attorney.

"But trust me Dawn," Wanda continued, "Tracy's gonna have to answer for this shit one day – believe that. GOD is watching and one day she is gonna have to explain this shit to somebody. Actually the longer she waits to tell the truth, the worse she's gonna be. The guilt is gonna eat away at her health."

"Good, I hope it eats her ass up. She needs to feel some pain after what she's done to my husband."

"I'm just curious, what did Tracy's family have to say?"

"I think Jamal heard from one of her family members, but for the most part, I don't think they have said much."

"I'm not surprised – they probably feel like they have to defend her. I'm sure somebody in her family knew. If they didn't know for sure, I'll bet a few of them had a suspicion. Oh well - fuck'em all! As far as I'm concerned, they are either part of the solution or part of the problem."

Chapter 8 - *One Woman Too Many*

<u>Greg</u>

It was 9:00 p.m. on a Friday night, and I was bored. I'd been watching a Sanford and Son marathon, and was ready to get into something a little more exciting. I remembered seeing a flyer that said one of my favorite jazz musicians was performing at the House of Blues at 10:00 p.m. Within minutes I was in my closet looking for the perfect outfit.

While in route to the House of Blues, I popped in my Miles Davis CD to help me get in the mood. I pulled up to the entrance and relinquished my car keys over to the valet attendant. The attendants treated me like a celebrity when I pulled up because I was a regular visitor, and usually gave pretty good tips. I had also established a real good rapport with the bouncers. By slipping the bouncers a $20 bill even on the nights when the place wasn't packed, I was always whisked to the front of the line and let in before the regular customers.

I loved to bask in this superstar treatment. It helped increase the curiosity of all the cuties standing around outside waiting to get in. It was not uncommon for women to follow me around the club waiting for the perfect opportunity to ask my name, and what line of work I was in. I usually responded by saying I was an entrepreneur who invested in real estate and upstart technology companies. For most women this was enough to get their attention - I relied on my "game" and good looks to keep their attention.

While sitting at the bar waiting to receive the Long Island Iced Tea I'd ordered, I noticed a sexy sista walking my way...it was Lisa. Since running into each other in Tipitina's a decade earlier – we'd been involved in an off and on sexual relationship. The type of no strings attached relationship I liked.

"Long time, no see!" she said.

"Yeah I haven't seen or heard from you in nearly three months," I replied, as I looked her up and down.

I noticed that Lisa looked a little upset. She tried to look calm as she sipped on the drink she was holding, but it was obvious she was flustered.

"Yeah I know. I've been going through some things. I was gonna call you cause I need to talk to you about something."

"I was wondering what happened to you. I tried calling you for a few weeks, but after you didn't return my phone calls I decided to stop sweatin' you."

"That's not it. I wasn't tryin' to be a bitch or anything, but I've had a lot on my mind. How long are you going to be here tonight?"

"I'll be here until the end of the show."

"Good. I'm in here with my girlfriends, but I do need to talk to you before you leave tonight. I'll look for you, and if I don't see you I'll call you on your cell phone...but please don't leave before we've had a chance to talk."

"Cool!" I said as I surveyed the club looking for a new victim.

As Lisa walked away, I was feeling pretty proud of myself. I noticed how all of the men at the bar were salivating as they watched Lisa in her skintight dress. One guy even made the comment, "No disrespect dog, but that's one of the finest women in here tonight."

I had to play it like a "G", "Yeah, she okay," I replied with a smirk.

There were still thirty minutes before the show was scheduled to start so I decided to scope out the scenery. I saw two attractive ladies sitting at a table laughing, and instantly decided that one of them would be leaving with me.

The object of my desire was a beautiful sista with a short hairstyle. She wore a low cut dress, stilettos, and could pass for Regina King's twin sister. I gathered my thoughts, and approached the ladies at the table with the assurance of a true playa.

"Hello ladies? My name is Greg, what's yours?"

Initially, both ladies looked at me as if I was an alien. They both politely responded by giving their names.

"I'm Cheryl, and this is my friend Stefanie."

I was glad the ladies were classy enough to at least give me their names. I knew that I was running the risk of experiencing every guy's nightmare...approaching a woman and being quickly dismissed. My buddies and I often sat back, and laughed at guys who were left with that stupid look on their faces as they tried to casually walk away from the scene of their embarrassment. I had never had that happen to me, but I knew that even the biggest playas got shot down from time to time so I always tried to be mentally prepared.

I'd been eyeballing Stefanie, but as luck would have it, Cheryl was doing most of the staring and talking. I spent the next hour sitting at the table with the ladies. I felt like I was getting nowhere trying to talk to Stefanie so I reluctantly started paying more attention to Cheryl. Stefanie was gorgeous, but she was stuck up! As the night went on she would occasionally join in the conversation, but I could tell that she wasn't interested in me.

Just when I was preparing to throw caution to the wind and ask Stefanie to dance, Lisa walked past the table. She made it a point to stare at me, but I didn't see her because I was drooling over Stefanie. Cheryl began to sense that she was loosing my attention so she did what most women in this situation do...she "playa hated."

"Greg, is that your woman or something because she's been staring over here for the last five minutes? She's obviously tryin' to get your attention."

I excused myself from the table, and walked towards Lisa. I felt like I was finally getting close to breaking through Stefanie's ice shield, so my mind was racing trying to come up with the best way to get rid of Lisa.

Even though I was trying to "mack" on Stefanie, I could see that Lisa was looking pretty damn good. Even if I struck out with Stefanie, Lisa would be a hell of a consolation prize. In true playa fashion, I wanted to get rid of Lisa, but keep my options open just in case.

"Lisa what's wrong with you?" I asked.

"Greg, my friends and I are about to leave, but I really need to talk to you."

"Well give me a call tomorrow. Maybe we can get together later on in the week."

"I would prefer to talk to you face-to-face. Is it okay if I come to your place tomorrow?"

"That's cool. Stop by around 4:00 p.m."

Mission accomplished. I'd successfully dealt with Lisa by setting up the booty for tomorrow, and making it look like a casual conversation. I took one last peek at Lisa's hourglass shaped figure as she walked away, and then I turned around and started walking back towards the table. Much to my dismay, Stefanie and Cheryl were gone.

It was 2:45 p.m. on Sunday, and I was preparing to watch the New Orleans Saint's receive another beat down. As I sat there devouring my chips and beer, Lisa called to tell me that she would be stop by in an hour. That gave me just enough time to shit, shower, shave, get the living room cleaned up, get the Best of Sade CD cued up, and clean up my bedroom. I knew that my encounters with Lisa were usually marathon sessions so I swallowed my last Viagra pill.

One hour later, I was finished preparing for my booty call. I'd just picked up my dirty underwear off of the bathroom floor when Lisa rang the doorbell. As I opened the door I noticed that she looked extremely nervous. At that moment, Sade's seductive voice (or melancholy depending on who you ask) began to engulf the living room:

"This may come, this may come as some surprise, but I miss you; I can see through all of your lies, but still I miss you."

Yeah, it was about to be on like popcorn...or so I thought. I invited her in and told her to make herself comfortable.

"You want something to drink? I got some Chardonnay," I asked.

"No thank you. I'll just take a glass of water."

When I returned into the living room with the glass of water I noticed that Lisa had her face covered with the palms of her hands. I could hear her crying, so I immediately turned down the volume of the CD player and asked, "Lisa what's wrong?"

When she heard my voice she started crying uncontrollably. This lasted for about three minutes; finally Lisa regained her composure.

"Greg, I've wanted to talk to you for a while now, but I didn't know what to say."

"What's got you so upset?"

Lisa wiped her face with the sleeves of her jacket and continued.

"You haven't seen or heard from me in the past month or so because I've been in Baton Rouge living with my aunt. I just needed to get away from here for a while."

I was starting to get nervous so I asked again, "Is everything okay?"

"I needed to talk to you," Lisa mumbled as she looked at me.

Suddenly, I knew what she was about to say. Just my luck – another knuckle headed woman trying to give me a damn charge. Well I was ready to tell her the same speech I gave Bianca – *I told you I don't want any kids!* Once I realized where this was leading, my patience became short. I needed her to spit the shit out, and then get the hell out of my house.

"Look Lisa, I'm trying to be patient, but you need to hurry up and tell me whatever it is you're trying to say."

She could tell from the tone in my voice that it was time to say what was on her mind, so she drank the water that I gave her, took a deep breath, and then spit it out.

"Greg, about a week after we last had sex I went to the doctor to have a check-up. A week later my doctor called me, and asked me to come in to speak to him. Greg, he told me that I am HIV positive." Lisa paused for a moment and then continued. "You need to go get checked. I realize I should have told you sooner, but when I initially found out I was in a state of shock for about a month. It wasn't until I had come to grips with my condition that I started thinking about whom I had slept with. That's when I thought about you..."

"Bitch I didn't give you HIV! As a matter of fact, I got tested last year." I yelled.

"I'm not saying you gave me the disease. I know who gave it to me, and I've already talked to him. I just found out that the guy who gave it to me is bi-sexual, but I didn't know before. If I had known he was bi-sexual I would have never started sleeping with you again. Greg, please listen to what I'm saying; you may have gotten tested last year, but you need to get tested again. I'm moving to Phoenix, Arizona on tomorrow to get as far away from New Orleans as possible. This is why I needed to talk to you so bad."

I stood up and walked towards my living room window.

"Lisa get out of my house," I said in a relatively calm voice.

"Greg, I'm so..."

"I said get the fuck out of my house!"

Lisa stood up and walked towards the front door. As she walked out of the door she looked back, and apologized to me once again for waiting so long to tell me. Her last image of me was my staring at the floor. But what she couldn't see were the tears forming in my eyes.

After Lisa left, I sat on my sofa with my mouth open. I was literally frozen with fear. I couldn't believe what I'd heard. There were times when I didn't use a condom, but since I only dealt with "divas" and not your typical "hood rats" I assumed that I didn't have anything to worry about. My ignorance had gotten the best of me.

To some degree, I thought I was immune to the disease...after all, I wasn't gay and I wasn't a junkie. I sat in that same spot for another two hours. From the moment Lisa left my apartment, a million things crossed my mind:

This can't be true; I got to get tested! Do I really want to know? How many people have I slept with since I last hooked up with Lisa? Should I call them or should I just let them think they got it from someone else? Should I call Jamal and tell him? Is my mama looking down on me right now? Is this GOD's way of punishing me for not being a good dad to my kids?

I spent the rest of the night getting drunk and high. I went to sleep on the floor in my living room next to the glass of water I'd given to Lisa. As I lay sprawled on the floor I glanced at the glass and thought to myself:

"That BITCH!"

Two days later, I visited a local HIV testing center to get tested. When I pulled up I recognized a guy leaving the building, so I sat in my car until the man was out of sight. I was wearing a pair of shades and a jogging suit with the hood pulled over my head. I was more concerned about being seen going into the building, and less concerned about what awaited me. My behavior was symbolic of an attitude that is all too common within the African-American community...getting tested for HIV is still considered taboo. As the disease continues to become more prevalent within the African-American community, the realization that HIV is no longer a "gay" disease is enough to cause many African-Americans to avoid testing all together.

As I walked into the building I saw a little old lady at the receptionist desk. The lady was extremely kind, and reminded me of my late grandmother. She gave me some forms to fill out and told me to be seated until she called my name.

I looked around and saw that I was the only person in the waiting room. I started to relax, and begin to feel like I was getting worried for nothing. After all, there is no guarantee that I was infected even though I'd slept with Lisa. I completed the paperwork and brought it back to the receptionist. I sat back down and waited for my name to be called.

Approximately ten minutes later, a nurse came into the waiting area and called my name. I was talking on my cell phone with my back to the nurse. When I turned around to respond to my name being called my mouth dropped...the nurse calling my name was none other than Stefanie - the girl from the nightclub.

We stared at each other for a few seconds. I was embarrassed as I hesitantly walked towards Stefanie. Stefanie treated me as if she had never met me before. She led me into a treatment room, and started reading my paperwork – avoiding eye contact.

She drew my blood and went over the process with me like I was a complete stranger. After awhile, the silent treatment seemed rather stupid to me so I decided to break the ice.

"Hello to you too!" I said sarcastically.

"Hi Greg. I didn't speak sooner because you seemed embarrassed that I saw you here," she replied.

"Actually I am a little embarrassed."

"Why?" she asked.

"Because! Who wants to be seen in an HIV clinic?"

Stefanie paused for a second and then looked at me annoyingly.

"That's the problem with black folk; we're more concerned about public perception than our own health. Every black person should be getting checked these days. There are so many closet bi-sexual men and junkies out there that black women don't know where their men have been. And straight black men don't know if the women they're dealing with have hooked up with one of those "down-low" brotha's."

Stefanie's words hit me like a ton of bricks. She didn't realize it, but she was *preaching to the choir*. I could have been the poster boy for what she was describing. Stefanie started spouting numerous statistics about HIV in the black community, but I could barely hear her. My mind started drifting, and once again I begin to think about the potential fallout from a "positive" test:

Who did I sleep with after Lisa? How will I tell them? What will Bianca say once she finds out?

I snapped out of my trance when I heard Stefanie say, "Well Greg, you should be getting your results in about two weeks."

"Damn I gotta wait two weeks?" I asked.

Stefanie simply shrugged her shoulders and walked out of the room. As she closed the exam room door she turned to me and said, "If your results come back negative, maybe we can do lunch." Stefanie gave me a wink, and then closed the door.

I stood in the treatment room smiling like a kid locked inside of a candy store. I'd spent an entire night trying to talk this woman in the club, and she treated me like I had smallpox. Now that my mind is on a million other things, she decides to give me some play. Normally I would have pulled one of my "playa" moves and told her "thanks, but no thanks." But, all I could think when I looked at Stefanie was, *damn she's fine!*

As I walked out of the treatment room, and back into the lobby I had a confident smile on my face. I glanced over at the little old lady sitting at the receptionist desk, and then smiled and gave her a wink. Much to my surprise, the old lady smiled back and said, "She's a cutie ain't she?" I couldn't hide my embarrassment as I nodded in agreement.

Stefanie's little flirtatious comment made my trip to the clinic a little less nerve wrecking. As I exited the building, and headed towards my car I started to put my shades on, but decided not to. Stefanie's comments about getting tested made a lot of sense to me. Suddenly, I was no longer ashamed about getting tested; as a matter of fact, I wore my testing as a badge of honor.

I drove away from the clinic with a newfound confidence. I had confronted my fears about being tested, and had started convincing myself that everything would be okay. Everything was out of my hands at that point, and I refused to worry about something that I had no control over.

I decided that I would abstain from sex until my test results came back. I quickly found that this was easier said than done. I couldn't remember the last time I had gone two weeks without some form of sex. The more I tried not to think about it, the more offers came my way.

The day after getting my HIV test, I got a phone call from three different women. With everything going on in my life I'd forgotten that it was my birthday. Each of the women called to ask if they could give me my present in person. I bravely turned down each offer, and was feeling pretty damn proud of myself. This HIV test was forcing me to tap into discipline and restraint that I didn't know I had.

The decision to abstain from sex also forced me to reflect on my life, and the behavior that led to my current situation. I started thinking about the women

I'd slept with over the years – I actually tried to count, but that was a joke. I could barely remember to visit my mom's gravesite on her birthday – it was a waste of time trying to remember all of my sexual conquests. I could remember faces, figures, and the locations of our encounters, but many of the names simply eluded me.

I remembered having sex with one woman in the bathroom stall at a sports bar...but I forgot her name. I remembered hooking up with a married woman whose husband was a big time businessman and always gone on business trips. I met her in a park one day, and screwed her on the sliding board once the sun had gone down and the park was empty. By far, one of the wildest encounters in my life...but I'd forgotten her name. I remembered going to a strip club once when I lived in Los Angeles, and leaving with two strippers who happened to be roommates. Those women took me on a ride I'd never forget. It was my first ménages a trios...but I couldn't remember their names.

I realized that over the years I had been indulging in nothing more than meaningless sex. I may have enjoyed it at the time, but I soon forgot about my encounters. Rarely did I sleep with any woman more than three times because for me that was too much like a relationship.

I knew that I was taking a risk when I engaged in this senseless sex, but I couldn't stop. I had come to the conclusion years earlier that I was a sex addict. Rather than seek help for my obsessive and potentially harmful behavior, I decided to live with my problem. I figured that if I had to have an addiction I'd rather it be sex and not drugs or gambling.

During those two weeks I gave serious thought to the changes I would make in my life. I decided to contact Bianca and apologize to her for the irresponsible way I had been acting, and tell her that I was ready to be a dad to Mya.

Second, I would contact Stefanie and try to see if we could work on becoming friends. For the first time in my life, I was ready to be in a monogamous relationship. I had been smitten with Stefanie from the moment I saw her, and in my gut I knew that if I were to settle down, it would have to be with someone like her – confident, good career, attractive, and capable of putting me in my place.

Last but not least, I decided that I would contact Jamal and apologize for things I had said. I knew that if I were going to really change my life, I would need to extend an "olive branch" his way.

True to form, once I made up my mind about what I was going to do I did not hesitate to get it done. I called Bianca for three consecutive days and left messages on her cell phone and home phone number asking her to give me a call. It had been months since I left her standing on my porch with our daughter, and she was still angry with me. By the third day I was begging Bianca to give me a call.

Bianca knew that I had never made much of an attempt to be a part of Mya's life so she figured that if I was being this persistent I was probably serious this time. She finally returned my call and needless to say she had a lot to get off her chest.

"Tell me one reason why I should let you be a part of Mya's life," Bianca demanded. "You haven't done a damn thing for her in all this time, now all of a sudden you want to be a daddy."

"Look Bianca I know you're mad, but I..."

"No Greg you don't know shit. All you know is how to make a baby. You don't know anything about being a daddy. You walk around here like your shit don't stink, wearing Rolex watches and $200 shoes, and all the while you got a baby you don't even take care of. You are one sorry mutha fucka!"

I remained silent. I knew I had this ass-chewing coming. Rather than try to argue I decided to shut up, and let Bianca get her anger out. Bianca yelled at me for another five minutes - I didn't say a word. Everything Bianca was saying was true. I knew that I had been a "deadbeat" dad – if this was my punishment then I was prepared to take it like a man.

Bianca realized that I wasn't responding, and was somewhat confused about what to do once she started repeating her insults. Finally she asked, "Well Mr. "*My Shit Don't Stink*" Johnson, why are you so quiet? Any other time you have a lot to say."

I humbly responded, "I don't have anything to say because you're right. I haven't been actin' like a real man, and I know it. All I want now is an opportunity to make up for lost time."

My response was met with silence. I could hear Bianca sniffling and crying. When I heard her whimpering my eyes begin to fill with tears. At that moment I could hear Mya in the background.

"Despite what you've done to her - this child worships the ground you walk on. Greg, don't let my baby down." Bianca said as she openly sobbed.

Before I knew it tears were running down my face. I could hear Mya trying to wrestle the phone from Bianca so that she could talk to me. I really wasn't ready to talk to her because I didn't feel worthy. I hadn't rehearsed my lines and had no idea what to say. Suddenly Mya got on the phone.

"Hey daddy!" she said.

I was speechless. I'd never known the impact the word "daddy" could have once spoken by a child.

"Hey baby girl. I miss you," I responded.

"I miss you too," with the innocence that only a child could display.

"Well, I would like to see you this week," I said as I fought hard to hold back the tears.

"I wanna see you," Mya responded, not bothering to try to hide her excitement.

Mya gave Bianca the phone back and left out of the room. Bianca picked up the phone, and we started making arrangements. We agreed that Bianca would bring Mya to my house two days later (Saturday morning), and the three of us would go to breakfast and spend the day together.

For the first time in a long time, Bianca and I finished a discussion on a good note. For the first time in my adult life I felt proud of myself. I had just taken the first step towards changing my life, and I was ready to take a few more.

I decided to call the clinic to see if I could set up a date with Stefanie. Although my test results had not yet returned, I knew that they would be in soon. I was feeling brave after my encounter with Bianca, so I figured I had nothing to lose. As I reached for the phone it started to ring...my mood would suddenly change.

The voice on the phone belonged to an elderly lady who seemed somewhat hesitant to speak. I said hello three times before the lady introduced herself and stated the reason for her call. The lady was a representative of the clinic, and she asked me to come in to hear the results of my HIV exam. I felt like my heart was about to come through my chest. There was something in the ladies tone that reeked of bad news.

I told the lady that I would come to the clinic to get my results the next day. As I sat on my sofa I felt paralyzed. I had to use the bathroom, but I simply couldn't move. Within a five-minute time frame my emotions had gone 360 degrees - from sad to happy to sad again. No matter how much I tried to snap out of it, I couldn't. No matter how much I tried to think positive, I felt in my gut that my results would be bad.

That next day I went to the clinic and upon entering into the waiting room I witnessed a scene that would only worsen my mood. I saw a very attractive young lady sitting on the floor in a corner of the waiting room crying uncontrollably. Stefanie was kneeled down next to the lady attempting to console her, but her efforts seemed futile. Stefanie saw me walk in, but didn't have time to acknowledge me. Her lack of acknowledgment didn't bother me because after witnessing the condition of that young lady I was tempted to turn around and leave.

I stopped in my tracks and surveyed the room. I noticed a second couple sitting side-by-side holding a bible praying. I could feel in my gut that this was not going to be one of my better days.

I made my way to the counter, and told the receptionist that I was asked to come in to get my results. It was the same old lady at the counter, but this time she wasn't as pleasant. She wasn't rude to me, but I noticed that she seemed to avoid making eye contact with me. I sat down and waited for my name to be called.

I sat quietly and watched as Stefanie helped the young lady off of the floor, and escorted her to a secluded room much like the one that I had originally had my exam done in. Approximately five minutes passed, and then a gray haired black lady wearing a lab coat entered into the waiting room holding a chart. The lady called my name without looking up, and immediately turned around and headed back down the long hallway that lead to her office. I found the woman's behavior to be rude, and when we sat down in her office I found her introduction to be rather curt.

"Hello my name is Dr. Sanborn. Please sit down so that we can get right to your results...Mr. Johnson as you know you are here today to go over your HIV results."

I didn't feel like sitting through any speeches so I boldly asked, "What does it say?"

The doctor gave me a look of annoyance. She made me feel like we were in a play, and I was saying my lines to fast causing her to lose her place. She placed my file on her desk and leaned back in her big leather seat. She crossed her arms, and gave me a stare that was as cold as her initial introduction.

"Mr. Johnson, according to your test result, you have contracted the HIV virus. Now there are several treatment techniques that we can explore, but first I need to know all of your sexual partners within the last 12 months. Also, I need to know if you have been involved in any intravenous drug usage, and if so, who have you shared a needle with?"

I didn't respond verbally. I could hear what the doctor was asking me, but I couldn't open my mouth. I was in a state of shock, and all I could do was shake my head in response to her questions. Prior to my visit I'd attempted to prepare myself emotionally, but I quickly learned that there is no way to prepare oneself for this type of tragic news. I could feel my eyes filling up with water, but I refused to breakdown in front of this rude and insensitive doctor. I couldn't see myself reacting the way that young lady did in the waiting room.

I answered all of the doctors' questions, and made arrangements to receive further treatment, before I walked out of the doctor's office. As I re-entered the waiting room I noticed that there was no one there. Even the receptionist was gone. I slowly walked towards the front entrance. With each step I could feel myself getting weak. I fought back my tears until I got home, but before I could make it from my front door to my sofa I begin to cry profusely. I fell to one knee, and leaned my back against the front door. There I sat for the next hour. I cried until my eyes hurt and my head throbbed.

It took awhile, but eventually I pulled myself up off of the floor, and made my way into my bedroom. I went into the bathroom and puked up a week's worth of dinner before making it to my closet to retrieve the shoebox where I kept my weed. I carefully sliced open and gutted a cigar and poured a generous amount of weed inside. Once I rolled my blunt to my liking I walked into the kitchen and grabbed an unopened pint of Hennessey and a small glass.

As I staggered back towards my bedroom I glanced at the mantle over my fireplace, and saw the picture I'd taken with Mya years earlier. I went and grabbed the picture, placed it under my armpit, and walked into my bedroom. Once inside, I laid my back against my headboard and stared at the picture for a few minutes. I poured the Hennessey in the glass, lit the weed, and tried to relax. My mind was clear of thoughts. I was on a mission to mentally escape my current circumstances, and I had just boarded the plane. Whether or not I would ever land was yet to be determined.

Chapter 9 - Closure

Greg

Saturday morning came and the chirping of birds outside of my bedroom window awakened me. I made my way to the kitchen to make a pot of coffee, and was startled when the phone rang. I wasn't accustomed to getting calls before 9:00 a.m., and had no idea who it could be. Much to my surprise it was Stefanie. She'd got my home phone number from my records, and decided it was time to stop playing hard to get. I was glad that she was finally showing some interest in me, but the news I'd received the day before made it hard for me to be happy about anything.

When I answered the phone I was very defensive. "What?"

"Hello Greg?" she hesitantly asked, wondering if she'd dialed the wrong number.

"Yeah this is Greg."

"Hi, this is Stefanie from the clinic. Did I catch you at a bad time?"

"Stefanie lets not play games; if you looked at my file to get my phone number than I know you saw my test results. I'm goin' through a lot right now; I don't need anyone insulting my intelligence."

"That wasn't my intention. Yes, I know about your test results."

"So why are you calling...looking for the details so that you can run and tell your girlfriend Cheryl."

"I have no intention of telling Cheryl your business. I just wanted to call and check on you. I know we don't know each other that well, but I am here for you if you need me."

"Thanks, but I'm gonna have to figure this one out for myself."

"I understand that too. What are you doing this evening? I was wondering if maybe we could get together. I'm free this weekend, and I figured maybe we could grab dinner and a movie."

I was surprised at Stefanie's call and proposition. At first I figured that she was just trying to be nice. This thought disturbed me because I didn't want to be viewed as a charity case. Nonetheless, I really liked her. She was one of the few women I'd met that made me work for it. I sensed that she liked me, and I knew that I'd made it clear to her that I was interested. On top of that, she knew his test results and still called me. I could feel in my gut that there was something different about this woman, and although I was embarrassed that she knew I'd tested positive, I was still eager to get to know her.

I was about to commit to dinner and the movies when I remembered that I'd made plans to see Mya and Bianca. Images of leaving Bianca and Mya standing at the front door years earlier while I slept with Lisa raced across my mind. It was my immaturity on that day that placed me in my current predicament, and I was determined to learn from my mistakes. Besides, now that I was faced with my own mortality, I was committed to making positive changes before my time ran out.

"You know what Stefanie, I am flattered that you would offer to hang out with me, but I've already made plans to be with my daughter and I'm gonna stick to them," Greg said.

"Oh that's sweet," she responded.

"Trust me, I am no where close to being a candidate for dad of the year - I just need to make things right with my daughter and her mother."

"Trust me I understand. Like Jill Scott said, "sometimes we all gotta swim up stream." I respect the fact that you want to hang out with your daughter. Handle your business. Oh yeah, for the record, I do like you and I still want to do dinner and a movie. Maybe we can hook up on Sunday if you're not busy."

This didn't seem real. I was HIV positive and she knew it. I was supposed to be sprawled across the floor screaming right about now, but all I could think about was this nice woman that had just come into my life.

"If you bout it, than I'm bout it!" I replied as I smiled for the first time in what seemed like forever. "I assume this is your home phone number on my caller i.d. box?"

"Yes, and you'd better use it," she replied.

"Cool! I'll call you tomorrow evening around two o'clock, and you can give me your address so that I can come pick you up."

I hung up the phone and started to smile – something I didn't think I could do after receiving the worst news since being told my mother died. I opened the curtains on the window over my kitchen sink, and let the beautiful sunlight shine through. Make no mistake about it; I was still scared and saddened by my test results. But, for some reason I wasn't feeling as upset as I thought I would.

As I sat at my kitchen table I started to think about a sermon I'd seen a televangelist give a few weeks earlier. The preacher talked about how GOD will allow you to hit rock bottom forcing you to humble yourself and come to him. I was definitely feeling humble at that point, and I felt the need to do something I hadn't done in years...pray! As the rich aroma of the coffee percolating in my coffee pot filled the air, I closed my eyes and begin to pray:

GOD, I know that I haven't come to you enough, and I know that I have lived my life rather foul, but I can't change the past. I guess this illness is the reaping what I've sown. All I ask at this point GOD is that you allow me to clear my conscious about all of the hurtful things I've done to people. I just want to make things right with the people I love. GOD please forgive me for my sins, and watch over me the way I know that you always have. In Jesus name I pray to you. Amen!

I opened my eyes and poured myself a cup of steaming hot coffee, and then I went outside to grab my newspaper. While I was outside I also went to my mailbox and grabbed my mail, which had been sitting there for two days. I went back inside and placed the newspaper and all of my mail on the kitchen table. After thumbing through a few bills I came across one of my monthly magazine subscriptions. It was Movers and Shakers Magazine. The cover page was entitled: "40 Professionals Under the age of 40 Doing Big Things!"

My mouth dropped when I saw Jamal's picture on the cover. His businesses were doing extremely well – he was earning six figures a year and counting.

I immediately opened up the magazine and read the entire article. I was so proud of him that I had water in my eyes. I reflected back on all those years that we sat in my bedroom and smoked, drank, talked about life and women, and laughed at each other's corny jokes. But my mood became somber when I thought about our last argument at the airport, and the cold way I'd treated him.

I'd taken the first steps with Mya, Bianca, and Stefanie – it was time to take the first step with Jamal. I drank the rest of my coffee as I tried to decide how I was going to deal with my former best friend.

Jamal

It had been six months since I'd sent Jada back home to live with Tracy. During that time I felt like I'd been on an emotional roller coaster. I utterly despised Tracy for the way she handled things. Ironically, it wasn't the anger of being lied to about the paternity that was irritating me. Now I was angry because Tracy was going around telling anyone who'd listen that I'd rigged the test. As far as I was concerned, her inability to be a "woman" and acknowledge what she'd done to me was the ultimate insult, but accusing me of rigging the test results was an even more cowardly act...and she was doing it with ease.

My resentment for Tracy grew even more after I had lunch with a group of females – very opinionated females. I headed to North Dallas to meet with three of my good friends Angie Lawton, Verlinda Burnstorm, and Marie Thompson – they were partners in a very successful real estate firm. I befriended them once I moved to the area; they were all on the cover of Movers and Shakers Magazine with me.

While eating lunch at Chipolte, they asked about my family.

"How are Dawn and the kids?" Marie asked.

"They're fine," I replied in a dull tone.

"How's your daughter? She's graduating this year isn't she?" Verlinda asked as she picked through her grilled chicken salad.

It was the first time anyone had asked me about my "daughter" since the DNA test, and I really didn't know how to answer. A part of me wanted to pretend like Jada was still my "daughter", but the truth of the matter was – biologically she wasn't. Emotionally I was still attached, but our lack of communication was beginning to have an affect on my feelings. I even had a hard time using the word "daughter" - I begin to stutter.

"What's wrong? Is she okay?" Angie asked.

I paused for a moment and then proceeded to tell them about the DNA test. I started from the day I found out – moved through the day I confronted Tracy – talked about how I allowed Jada to return to live with me – and finished with the day I sent her back to New Orleans.

They all listened intently as looks of astonishment covered their faces. Angie knew that this was a very sensitive topic so she chose her words carefully.

"Do you think it was wise to send that child home?" asked Angie, who always seemed to be the most diplomatic of the three.

"But..." I attempted to defend my position but Angie cut me off.

"But nothing Jamal! At the end of the day, that's still a child. Is she immature? Yes! Was her mother dead wrong for what she did and how she handled things afterwards? Yes! But, at the end of the day you have to be the bigger person," she said.

"Angie I'm tired of always being the one who has to take the damn high road. They both owe me some respect," I barked causing the couple at the next table to look over.

"I agree!" Marie chimed in. I always liked Marie's feisty attitude. She was the smallest person at the table, but she had the biggest bark. "I'm glad you sent her little ungrateful ass back to her mama. Once Tracy starts treating her like shit again I'll bet she'll wish she'd given you some respect."

"You're right about that," Verlinda added; she wasn't as feisty as Marie, but she was a close second. "Jamal, the apple doesn't fall far from the tree. That child sounds like she's just like her mama."

"You are absolutely right. It sounds like both mother and daughter are just alike," interjected Angie. "They both are ungrateful and don't appreciate you – they probably never will. However, you remember this - to those whom much is given, much is expected. You have been blessed with a more mature mind than them. Whether you like it or not, you have to take the high road."

I had a lot of respect for Angie's ability to look at issues very strategically so I listened. She was good fusing Christian principle into her arguments. But, I still didn't agree.

"It sounds like you are condoning what she did to me," I commented.

"No I'm not," Angie replied. "But Jada is still your daughter Jamal. Regardless of what that test may have shown that is still the child you helped raise – don't lose sight of that."

There was an eerie silence at the table. Angie was the voice of reason that is always needed during any gripe session. As she spoke I frowned and sighed, but I listened intently.

"At the end of the day, I think it's important that you not lose sight of the fact that GOD does not make mistakes. You were placed in that child's life for a reason. No other man but you. GOD could have given the responsibility of raising that child to someone else, but he chose you. It may feel like your efforts were for naught, but I don't believe that they were. You are going to have to take solace in the fact that you did the job GOD put you here to do."

"No disrespect to you Angie, but you are a woman, and you'll never know how much it hurts to be lied to like this," I stated in a tone that signaled I was through listening.

"Jamal I'm not condoning what she did, and I know that I'll never be able to understand what you're feeling. All I'm sayin'..."

My temper got the best of me and I interrupted Angie mid-sentence.

"Let me ask you this! As a woman, can you explain to me how a woman can just lie about something this devastating?"

"Jamal to be honest with you - I don't know. I know that my conscience wouldn't allow me to lie to a man about something as serious as paternity. The only thing I can conclude is that you put her on the spot in front of her fiancée and she felt that her only way out was to lie so that he wouldn't get mad at her – now she has to stick with it," Angie replied.

"Whatever!" Marie yelled. "I'll tell you how a woman can lie about something like this. Because she never thought you'd find out. Angie, you're sittin' here acting like you've never heard of something like this. I am 46 years old, and I can think of at least three different times in my adult life when I heard about some woman lying about the paternity of her child. Jamal, this shit is more common than men realize. I'm sorry, she ain't gonna get the benefit of the doubt from me. I have a very handsome and intelligent son whom I adore. If I found out some woman did this to him, they'd have to strap me down in one of those white jackets that they put those crazy people in."

"That's okay girlfriend, I'd help your crazy ass break out and we'd go beat that tramp down," said Verlinda, causing everyone at the table to laugh.

The laugh was needed because the scene was starting to get tense. After a few seconds of silence Marie continued, "Seriously Jamal, once the lie survived for a few years, she figured she was home free. The shit really isn't that difficult to figure out – she underestimated you!"

"I agree," said Verlinda. "It was her plan to take that lie to her grave. What's sad is that she will probably deny it until she's old and gray. Some people tell a lie so long that eventually they start to believe it themselves."

"So Angie, are you suggesting that he shouldn't have confronted her?" Marie asked.

"I'm saying that maybe he should have got her alone and then showed her the test results. Maybe she would have reacted differently, but now she's in defense mode. The only thing she cares about is trying to save face. Right now, she's more concerned about how she's viewed by family members and friends."

"So fuck what I feel – right? I'm only the nigga who's provided support for eighteen years! Do you know she had the audacity to expect me to finance that child's college education and buy her a car for graduation?"

"That's bullshit!" Marie blurted out. "You've already paid emotionally and financially! Her ass doesn't have the decency to tell the truth now that the results are in, but she expects you to finance a car and spend another forty to fifty thousand dollars on college tuition? Jamal, I hope you cursed that bitch out? If you didn't, give me her phone number so I can call and curse her ass out!"

"I'm witcha sista," said Verlinda. "We should go down there one day and snatch her ass up by the neck. That's what I would do if someone lied on my brother. Jamal what did your relatives in New Orleans do when they found out?"

"Don't even get me started on that," I said as the look of annoyance engulfed my face.

"Were they upset?" Marie asked.

"My siblings were angry, but there are some people in my family who have disappointed me."

"What did they do?" Angie asked.

"I got cousins down there that are helping her spread lies that I falsified the DNA test."

"WHAT!!" yelled Marie and Verlinda - Angie just shook her head in disbelief.

"Yep – she's telling people that I had the test performed by some people I know that work at a hospital. She's also claiming that the test isn't authentic because she wasn't there to offer a DNA sample."

"So tell me Jamal - what did you expect?" asked Angie.

"I don't know, but right about now I'm not sure what bothers me the most – the fact that she deceived me for all those years or the fact that she has tried to make me look like the "bad guy" rather than taking responsibility for what she did."

"Would it matter if she took responsibility?" asked Angie. "It wouldn't change the results."

"It wouldn't change the test results, but I wouldn't feel like I was being kicked while I'm down. Telling everyone I rigged the test is like spitting in my face."

"I understand," said Verlinda. "She's compounded the problem by trying to make you look bad."

"I don't know what you expect from her," said Marie. "If her ass is trifling on Monday, she's gonna be trifling on Friday! Brotha, you'd have a better chance of winning the lottery than trying to get Tracy to tell the truth."

"She can't tell the truth because she doesn't know the truth," said Verlinda.

"HELLO!!!!" yelled Marie, as she and Verlinda gave each other a high-five.

"I'm not crazy – I know that there's a chance she had multiple partners and doesn't know who the real daddy is," I said.

"If she admitted that, could you handle it?" asked Angie.

"It would be hard, but at least I could bring some closure to this from an emotional standpoint. I would definitely have more respect for her," I replied.

"I'm still trying to figure out how in the hell you could rig a damn DNA test," said Marie as she sat back in her chair and placed her index finger to her temple. "That would mean that the Lab Technician and every person at the testing site who came in contact with those samples are helping you lie. We all know that no one – not black folk and damn sure not white folk - is gonna risk their job just to help your black ass rig a test. That's just dumb, and anyone who believes that is dumb! Secondly, she doesn't have to be present for the test – she carried the child for nine months so there's no question that she's the biological mother. The only thing that's in question is who the real daddy is. Only the child and the man need to be present during the test. If it was a requirement that everyone always be present, the police wouldn't be able to use DNA to solve those old murders or use it as evidence to get innocent people off of death row."

"Well Marie, she obviously found the right audience because people believe the stuff she's telling them," I replied.

Verlinda scratched her forehead and then asked, "What I wanna know is – even if it was possible to rig the test, why would anyone think you'd wait 18 years to do it? The smart thing to do would be to rig the test before you spent all of your money on the child.

Jamal, someone in your family has got to see how that doesn't make sense?"

"If they don't see it, it's because they don't want to see it. You know what they say, your family will turn on you quicker than your enemy," Angie mumbled.

"Shiiiit, often times your family is your worst enemy. The only people who would believe that foolishness are the people who had some other issue with you or some kind of deep down jealousy. They were lookin' for a reason to talk about you. Trust me, if it wouldn't have been this issue they would have found somethin' else," said Marie.

"I know that's right," said Verlinda as she pushed away her plate. "Unfortunately, the only time they're not your enemy is when they think they can get somethin' out of you. The moment they figure they can't get anything from you they'll feed your ass to the wolves...but I guess you know that by now Jamal."

Angie took a drink of her lemonade and said, "Jamal I know you don't want to hear this, but I'm your friend so I'm gonna tell you the truth. It sounds like Tracy has never respected you. She may have respected your money, but she never respected you. It also sounds like she is a troubled woman. Trust me, at some point she is gonna have to come to you and tell the truth – the guilt is gonna ruin her life. No matter how many lies she tells to try to justify her actions, GOD knows the truth. A lot of times we try to hide behind the fact that GOD forgives us of our sins...this is true. But, that doesn't exonerate us of the responsibility to do the right thing. GOD is going to speak to heart, and I believe he's going to use that child to do it. Every time she looks at Jada she's gonna have to think about what she did. Every time she looks at a father with his daughter she's gonna think about what she did. I don't care if she's watching a movie or in the aisle at Walmart, she's going to be reminded of how she handled this situation. Trust me, vengeance is the Lord's...you won't have to do a thing."

"Yeah, yeah, yeah - that may be true and that's a nice sentiment, but here's my opinion," said Marie. "At some point, Tracy and Jada are gonna realize that they messed up the best thing they had. As far as those family members that sided with her - just keep makin' that money and watch'em sweat!"

"Yeah I hear what you're sayin' Marie, but the betrayal still hurts...more than you know," I mumbled.

We raised glasses and said "Amen." Marie's remarks seemed like the perfect way to end lunch. We disposed of our drinks and got out of there.

I went home that evening thinking about that discussion. As much as I wanted to ignore some of Angie's comments something inside of me kept saying, *try one last time - extend the olive branch.*

While sitting at a stoplight, I called a cousin whom I knew could get in contact with Jada. I told my cousin to tell Jada that I wasn't angry with her, and that I wanted her to write me, e-mail, or call collect if need be. The cousin agreed to relay the message, but warned me that she couldn't guarantee that Jada would be receptive.

I hung up the phone feeling like I'd done the respectable thing. I wasn't sure how Jada would react, but I knew that I'd extended my last "olive branch."

I've never been a fan of the Texas heat, but after spending three days on a business trip in the heart of Arizona battling 100-degree temperatures, I was ready to go home.

My flight home was just as frustrating because I had to spend the entire four hour trip sitting next to a guy who needed a "Stick Up" placed under each arm.

When I arrived at my home, I made a mad dash for the bathroom and relieved myself of the awful

206

airline food I'd consumed. Afterwards, I went into my office to check my mail and answering machine.

As I opened the small refrigerator in my office to retrieve the already opened bottle of Kendall Jackson – Chardonnay, I pressed the message button on my answering machine and heard a voice that made me pause...it was Greg:

What's up Jay?! Look, I know it's been a long time since we talked. Give me a call because I really need to talk to you...it's very important. Peace!

Two days passed before Greg and I finally spoke. When we did speak to each other I could sense that something was terribly wrong with my old friend. Greg was crying and mumbling something about dying. I had never heard him this distraught. I told Greg that I would come to New Orleans in two days to be by his side.

I spent the next two days rearranging meetings in an effort to clear up my calendar. The one meeting I couldn't cancel was scheduled the day before I intended to leave town. The meeting was with my banker to discuss financing for a major business deal. As I was preparing to leave my home office and head towards the bank, I noticed that a new e-mail arrived. When I looked at the address block I could see that it came from Greg. I looked at my watch and saw that it was already 1:15 pm - my meeting was at 2:00 p.m. I knew that I didn't have time to read the e-mail so I decided to open it after my meeting.

Unfortunately, the meeting lasted longer than I expected. The bank was located in downtown Dallas, which meant I'd have to fight the rush hour traffic on my way home. I stopped at the supermarket on to pick up some items to go in my travel kit. By the time I arrived at home it was 7:00 p.m.

As I walked inside I could see Dawn sitting on the living room sofa. She was crying and before I could ask her what was wrong she walked towards me and gave me a hug. She squeezed me so tight that she hurt my shoulders.

"Baby what's wrong?" I asked.

"Sweetheart, Greg died today," Dawn replied as tears streamed down her face.

At first I thought I was hearing things, "What do you mean Greg's dead?" I asked. "I just talked to him the other day. As a matter of fact, I just got an e-mail from Greg this morning."

"Baby, Greg committed suicide today. Bianca called here to tell you. She found him when she brought Mya over to see him. He shot himself in the head. She said a policeman found a paper on the floor next to Greg that said he was HIV positive. Baby, I'm sorry to have to tell you this," Dawn said as she reached to hug me.

I don't remember much – only that I pushed Dawn's hands away and leaned against my living room wall and slid down to the floor. The news of Greg's death was a total shocker to me. I wanted to cry, but couldn't find the tears. All I could think about was our last conversation. He sounded as if he'd been crying and he mumbled something about dying.

I became angry with myself for not going to New Orleans sooner. Before I knew it, I was banging my head against the wall. With every blow the tears begin to flow. By the fifth blow I was crying uncontrollably. Images of Greg and I hanging out bombarded my mind. My best friend was gone.

After what seemed like hours, I managed to pick myself up and made my way into my office. I sat at my desk and stared at the unopened e-mail. When I opened it there was no writing. Just as I was about to delete it I noticed that there was an attachment. The attached letter read as follows:

What's up Jay? First let me say that I miss you more than you know. You may not realize it dog, but I've always admired you. As much as I hate to admit it, for a long time I've been jealous of you. You got your shit together and I respect that.

You'll be happy to know that I finally pulled my head out of my ass, and started doing right by Bianca and Mya. We hung out this weekend and I was supposed to see her again tonight.

Now that I got the easy shit out of the way, I need to tell you some things. First, I got diagnosed with HIV. Close your mouth nigga, I know you're shocked and shit. What can I say, I guess I had one woman too many. It's been hard, but I guess I'll just have to figure out a way to deal with it.

The second thing I want to talk to you about is really much harder than telling you I got HIV. I guess there is really only one-way to say it…I'm Jada's real father. Like I said, I've wanted to tell you this for years, but simply couldn't muster up the courage. That's why Tracy never gave you an explanation about the real father after you got the DNA results…she didn't want to tell you the truth. Tracy and I never had a relationship or anything - we just hooked up a few times in the summer of 1986.

Back when you first told me she was pregnant I tried to tell you she was lying. I knew she was lying because she had already confronted me, and I told her I wasn't taking care of a baby - you know how I was back then. I thought she was gonna get an abortion or give the charge to some other dude, I never knew she was going to stick you with that charge.

Remember the night you were at my house, and I was arguing on the phone with a woman? As we drove to the airport you asked me who the woman was - well Jay, the woman I was arguing with was Tracy. She wanted to tell you the truth, and I told her that we'd waited too late. That's why I snapped at you at the airport, my conscious was fucking with me. I knew I was wrong for doing that to you, and I was trying to push you away so that I wouldn't have to face you.

I don't ever expect you to forgive me for what I've done. I just want you to know that I have the utmost respect for you, and I will always love you like a brother. In an effort to make up for what I've done to you, I've left $75,000 in a safety deposit box. The key to the safety deposit box is taped to the back of my shoe box – yeah nigga you know my famous shoe box and you know where I keep it – ain't nothing changed. I want you to keep the money dog – you deserve it. I changed my insurance policy and made Bianca and Mya my beneficiaries. In the event the insurance company starts trippin' and decide they aint gonna pay – I want you to go ahead and sell my house and everything that's in it and give Bianca the money. I trust that you'll take care of my arrangements and see to it that my affairs and Mya are taken care of.

I've committed a lot of sins Jay, and now it's time for me to answer for them. Well man, I gotta go. I hope you keep making that money and doing big things. Do me a favor - let Mya know that I loved her. Unfortunately, I won't be around to say it to her. I'm tired dog - it's time for me to go be with my mama...if GOD lets me in.

Take care of yourself. Brothers 4 life!

Greg

As tears rolled down my face, I envisioned Greg and me partying, laughing, drinking, and even crying together. I was too consumed with grief over his death to really grasp his confession.

However, once I regained my composure, I thought about Greg's e-mail. Finally, the truth was out. It was Greg the entire time. Throughout the years I'd identified at least three guys who I thought could have been Jada's father: Sean – the guy from my high school; Darwin – her first husband; Mannie – my old friend who was in jail. Never in a million years did I suspect it was Greg. In hindsight, I shouldn't have been surprised. Women always threw themselves at Greg – I don't know why I thought Tracy was different.

Like most funerals - Greg's was sad. Throughout his entire life he'd always been the life of the party, and now the party was over. There were people standing wall-to-wall. As I stood up at the podium preparing to give the eulogy I saw men and women I hadn't seen in years.

Bianca sat on the front row crying uncontrollably as Mya sat next to her looking confused. A very attractive light skinned woman sat on the end of a middle row (it was Lisa; she stared at Greg's casket the entire funeral). I noticed a very pretty woman standing in the rear of the room wearing hospital scrubs (I later learned that the unidentified lady was Stefanie). Each person stared at Greg as his body lay there. Each person viewing him from a different perspective – literally and figuratively.

As I finished delivering the eulogy I saw a familiar face from the corner of my eye. Much like the other recognizable faces in the crowd - this person gazed at Greg like she was talking to him via mental telepathy. The woman sitting in the corner with the intense look on her face was Tracy.

After the services ended, I stood outside of the funeral home and said good-bye to many of the guests. Everyone knew that Greg and I had been best friends since high school. They treated me with the type of respect usually reserved for the immediate family members of the deceased.

I noticed Tracy walking across the street and heading towards a parked car. Two trucks that passed down the street temporarily blocked my vision. When the trucks passed I could see Jada sitting inside of the parked car. I quickly ended the conversation with some man I didn't even know, and was about to run over to Tracy's car. It wasn't my intent to make a scene – I just wanted to call a truce. Greg's funeral made me realize that life was too short to be arguing about things from the past.

As I moved towards the car I was stopped in my tracks. A woman blocked my path. It was the same cousin I'd called a week earlier.

I pointed at the car and told my cousin I was going to go over to talk to Jada.

"Jamal I've wanted to tell you, but when Greg died I thought it was inappropriate," she said as she grabbed me by the arm and pulled me away from the crowd.

I was confused and somewhat annoyed because I was trying to get to Tracy's car before she pulled off.

"Jamal please don't go over there. I talked to Jada last week and I told her what you said. She made it very clear to me that she doesn't want to talk to you."

"What do you mean she doesn't want to talk to me? After all the shit I did for..."

"Jamal that girl doesn't care – she's just like her mama."

The words compounded the grief that I was already feeling. For me, I felt like I had just been told of a second death. I made eye contact with Jada as the car pulled off. Greg was gone...and so was Jada.

One Year Later

"Hello Jamal," said the voice on the phone. The voice sounded distinguished.

"Hello – who am I speaking to?" I asked.

"It's Alex – Tracy's older brother."

I paused for a second. I hadn't spoken to Alex in nearly twenty years. The last time I'd seen him was back when he first found out Tracy was pregnant. He wanted to fight me because I'd impregnated his sister. I never had any issues with Alex. If I'd discovered that my little sister was pregnant while still in high school I would have reacted the same way. Still, to say I was surprised to hear his voice was an understatement.

"Alex – man it's been a long time since I've heard your voice. How have you been?"

"I've been fine man. Based on this Movers and Shakers magazine that I'm holding it looks like you're doing even better."

"I can't complain. I can't complain."

There was an uneasy silence for a few seconds. It was the type of silence that's usually followed by a bombshell.

"Look Jamal, I'm aware of what went down between you and my sister and I just want to apologize to you – I know that you must have been devastated."

"Yeah, I was devastated."

"Well, I am truly sorry. I've always been impressed by the way you took care of my niece."

"How is Jada?"

"Jada is still making questionable decisions. That's why I'm callin' you. Jada has decided that she's going to get married to that little boy she's been dating for the past few years."

"I'm not surprised. She's been itching to grow up before her time."

"I agree, but I think that this is a major mistake. I've tried to talk to her, but she won't listen."

"What is Tracy saying?" I asked.

"Unfortunately, my sister is encouraging this foolishness. I know that this may be a long shot, but I would like you to talk to her. I really believe that you are the only person she'll listen to."

"Man I don't know about that. I tried reaching out to her a year ago, and she didn't want to talk to me."

"I feel you, but I would appreciate it if you'd consider it."

"I doubt if she'll even get on the phone."

"I agree. That's why I was hoping you would drive down here. We could link up and I could take you where she is staying."

I spent the remainder of the night thinking about Alexs' phone call. I even discussed it with Dawn.

"So what do you think I should do?"

"I don't know - that's a tough one. The odds are great she's not going to listen to you. You will have made a wasted trip."

"I know, but I almost feel like I have to go. Jada is not ready for marriage – we both know that. I feel like I have to stop her from making the biggest mistake of her life."

"Well what is Tracy's position?"

"According to Alex, Tracy seems to be supporting this bullshit."

"I'm not surprised Jamal. Tracy and Jada can't live under the same roof too long. The sooner Jada's gone, the easier life is for Tracy."

"I agree. Still, I feel like I have to at least try. I would be beating myself up if I don't at least try to talk some sense into her."

"Well Jamal, if you feel like you have to go than I support your decision."

It only took an hour to reschedule all of my appointments so that I'd be free of any responsibilities for the remainder of the week. At five o'clock the next morning I was in my car heading down the highway to New Orleans.

I had eight hours to devise a plan of action, and six hours into my drive I still hadn't come up with anything. I knew that my approach had to be smooth and non-confrontational. I had to pretend like I was oblivious to her plans.

I arrived in New Orleans at 3:00 p.m. I went straight to Alexs' house where he and I came up with a plan on how we were going to ambush Jada. At about 6:00 p.m., he took me where she was located. We sat outside the house like two cops on a stakeout. Finally, Jada exited through the front door.

As she walked towards her car I jumped out of the car and walked as fast as I could without looking like a "purse snatcher" sneaking up behind a potential victim. When I called her name Jada turned around and looked like she'd seen a ghost.

"Hey daddy, you scared me!"

"Hello Jada. You got a second to talk?"

"Ahh yeah," she replied, her look and tone made it clear that she was uncomfortable with what was unfolding.

"Lets go up to the deli on the corner and get a bite to eat while we talk."

"O.K.," she replied hesitantly.

The deli was relatively empty. As we stood in line I looked at Jada from head to toe. Instantly, I was glad that I'd made the trip. This was my baby. This was my child. The pain of the test results had subsided. The feelings of betrayal were gone. This was my daughter – the child I helped raise.

We sat down at a table next to the window...bad move. Jada spent half the time staring out of the window and the other half talking to someone on her cell phone.

"So how have you been Ms. Jada?"

"I'm fine."

"Well, I've been thinkin' about you. How is everything going?"

"Everything is going well."

Jada's one-line answers made it clear to me that if this was going to be a productive discussion I was going to have to lead the way.

"Let me first say that I am sorry for my role in the "fall out" we had. In hindsight I should have swallowed my pride and feelings, and allowed you to stay in Dallas with me for the remainder of your senior year."

Jada seemed unmoved by my opening statement. She seemed to be daydreaming – until her cell phone rang.

"Excuse me, I need to take this call," she said as she left the table and walked into the ladies restroom.

A few minutes later Jada returned to the table. She placed the phone on the table and started staring out of the window again.

"As I was saying, I'm sorry about everything. I would really like to work on re-establishing our relationship."

"To be honest with you..." our conversation was interrupted once again by her cell phone. Once again she grabbed the phone and walked into the restroom.

When Jada returned this time she seemed to be a little more defiant...borderline curt.

"A lot is happening in my life," she blurted out.

"Like what?" I asked, sensing that this was the opportunity to get to the marriage topic.

"To be honest with you I've moved on to another phase of my life.'

"Excuse me – you've moved on? What does that mean Jada?"

"I've moved on. I've left those things in the past."

"Oh really?"

"Really."

I was floored by her attitude. This was the child that had respected me and listened to everything I said during the course of her life. Now, she was grown and she had no reservations about letting me know.

"Wow. I guess you're grown now; therefore, no one knows what's going to make you happy more than you do. Since you've apparently moved on to another phase of your life and left me in the past, tell me what else is happening with you."

"Well, I'm getting married."

"You're getting married? Who are you marrying?"

"I'm gonna marry my boyfriend Reggie."

"Jada, you do realize that's serious?"

"I know – we're ready."

"Honestly, I'm not surprised that you and Reggie are getting married. I'm surprised that you're doing it this soon, but I'm not surprised you're marrying him. Let me ask you something, are you pregnant?"

"No...that's the first thing everybody thinks."

"You must know that people are going to assume that. What does your mother have to say about this?"

"She is supporting it. As a matter of fact, she has already bought my dress."

"I can tell that your mind is made up on this so I'll leave it alone. If there is anything I can do to help please let me know. Do you need anything?"

"No, everything is taken care of," Jada replied.

"There is one thing that's confusing me – how can you get married and not have your father walk you down the aisle?"

Jada was silent. She started squirming in her seat and became very uneasy with the topic.

"Well Ms. Jada, it's clear that you have found someone else to stand in my place. Since I'm in town,

and the wedding is only three days away, is it alright
with you if I at least attend?"

Jada was silent. She avoided eye contact with me
the entire thirty minutes we sat there. I could tell by
the way her eyes darted around the room that she was
searching for a way to tell me I wasn't invited.

"So, should I take your silence as an answer?"

Jada looked down at the table and shook her head
in agreement.

"So you're telling me that I'm not invited to your
wedding?"

"To keep down confusion, I think it would be best
if you didn't come," she replied as she stared at
inanimate object over my left shoulder.

I could feel my emotions starting to take over.
Never had I felt so hurt, rejected, and disrespected.
Before I knew it, my feelings spewed out of my mouth
like floodwaters plunging through a broken dam.

"Let me get this straight – are you telling me that I
haven't done enough for you over the years to earn an
invitation to your wedding? When you first started
dating Reggie and your mother hated him, wasn't it
me that talked her into letting you see him? When
your mother put you out with nothing but the clothes
on your back, wasn't it me that took care of you?
When your mouth was full of rotten teeth wasn't it me
that got your teeth fixed so the kids wouldn't laugh at
you? Have you forgotten that I tried to hide the DNA
results from you? Have you forgotten that we were
both lied to for more than 17 years? In spite of all the
shit I've done for you, are you telling me I'm not good
enough to even come to your wedding? It's like that
Jada?"

After sitting there silently for a few seconds
looking like she was still trying to digest my little
diatribe, Jada slowly looked at me for the first time
that evening. Her face was almost emotionless as she
glanced at her cell phone, which was still ringing

uncontrollably. She adjusted her jacket, cleared her throat and said, "It's like that." Her voice never quivered, her tone remained low, and her face showed absolutely no emotion.

I on the other hand was battling to hold back my tears. I was the man here. I was the more mature adult. Yet, I was the one who was the emotional wreck. I could see her but she couldn't see me. I could feel her, but she wasn't feeling me. I wanted to hold her, but she was through with me. I was a thing of the past...she'd moved on to another phase of her life.

Conclusion

I feel like I've been driving for days. My eyes are playing tricks on me - it seems like the lanes on this highway are starting to merge. Still, I'm getting close to home. I just crossed the Louisiana/Texas border, but I'm so tired and distracted that I don't remember passing through Shreveport.

I put Jay-Z's new cd, _The Black Album_, in to add some life to this solemn experience, but I can't focus long enough to listen to any of the songs. I started to pop in some John Coltrane, but that won't work – the melodic rhythms of my man's saxophone will surely put my ass to sleep. The next thing you know, somebody would find this car lodged into one of the trees lining this highway.

One thing is for sure - I'm through crying. I'm all cried out. It's time to start worrying about me. It's time for me to start focusing on shit I can control.

When I get back to the "crib" the first thing I'm going to do is take everything out of Jada's old room and turn it into a home gym – I've wanted to do that for a while. Hell, I never use my gym membership anyway.

Shit, my mind is so messed up right now that I didn't even see that police car sitting at the top of that hill. The officer looked like he was staring right at me. The speed limit is 65, but I'm doing 80. I wonder if he noticed that I wasn't wearing my seatbelt. Well, he hasn't moved yet so I guess he didn't see...awwwwwh shit, here he comes! Just my luck, he's probably been sitting up there all day letting people pass by, and now he's gonna come mess with me.

The next exit is about a mile away; I wonder if I can make it before he catches up? He'd better step on it because if I make it to that exit he won't catch my black ass.

Damn! I was about to piss in my pants and he wasn't coming after me. It looks like he's stopping those white guys in that Corvette. Oh well, better them than me. He'll probably just give them a warning – my black ass would've been snatched out of the car like Rodney King.

That's foul. Those people weren't driving that fast but they are the one's who got pulled over. But I guess that's just how it is, sometimes when you try to do the right thing you still get shitted on...this I know. But that's cool because I'm about to use what Tracy and Jada did to me as motivation.

I heard some rapper say that the best way to get back at someone who dogs you out is to "blow up" - I agree with that. My businesses are already doing well, now I'm going to work even harder. I'm going to make them wish they had never treated me like this.

As a matter of fact, I think I'm going to buy that new Jaguar. Yeah, I'm gonna make both of their asses sick when they see me again. I'm going to make sure I spoil the hell out of my son because I know that his